I0822402

ELIZABETH JURADO

ILLUSTRATED BY DAVEY VILLALOBOS

Saygar the Magnificent

Second Editon: 2021

Interior Illustrations by Davey Villalobos
Edited by Rebecca Koch
Cover and Formatting: Streetlight Graphics

Published by Happy Lifestyles Online

Library of Congress Number: 2019916514

Hardcover ISBN: 978-1951203092
Paperback ISBN: 978-1-64570-597-0
Ebook ASIN: B07SQ7Z67C

Table of Contents

Ms. Kelly
3rd Grade

Dedication:

To my son Samuel and my mother, Estela, who helped immensely by listening to my Saygar ideas, developing storylines, and editing. Thank you for cheering on Saygar from the very beginning and through the many years. Thank you for never letting me give up despite the moments that made finishing seem so far.

Chapter 1
Show and Tell

MANY YEARS AGO, MY GREAT, great grandparents left Mexico in a covered wagon, crossed the Rio Grande River, and settled the Mateo family in El Paso, the pointy nose of Texas where the Lone Star State collides with New Mexico and Old Mexico. With the Rio Grande River only a few blocks from my home, the American and the Mexican ways of life come together.

In my neighborhood, the Mexican way of life had a way of taking over. There were other stories besides the classics like the Tooth Fairy, the boogeyman under the bed, and "an apple a day keeps the doctor away". My Great Grandma Mateo witnessed *La Llorona* weeping along the banks of the Rio Grande. A cousin of mine heard of a guy who knew of a guy who knew someone who had seen *El Cucuy* in the shadows under his bed. And my *Tía* Lucita and *Tia* Lupita never missed their yearly visit to the local *curandero* for their *limpia* in order to fight off evil spirits and potential curses.

I believed the stories when I was a little kid, but by first grade, I saw things differently. That was the year I caught my mom sneaking a quarter under my pillow. I had had my doubts when I heard that the Tooth Fairy was giving Georgie Jr., a kid from school, five dollars. Catching my mom just made it official: The Tooth Fairy was not real. From there, the stories fell like dominoes. The Tooth Fairy, *La Llorona*, *El Cucuy* were all fake, fake, fake. No one could change my mind--not until my third-grade year at Cadwallader Elementary School, at least. That was the year I became a true believer. I became one of those people, like Great Grandma Mateo, who would tell an unbelievable story.

My story begins with a simple walk to school, and an empty green ginger ale, two-liter bottle. My plan was to bring something for a show and tell kind of thing. I wasn't the kind of kid who liked to stand up in front of my class and talk. Ms. Kelly, my teacher, had spoken to my mom during my parent-teacher conference about my shyness and discussed the importance of "becoming more active in classroom discussions." She said something about how drawing me out of my comfort zone would help me interact better with my peers--Ms. Kelly's words, not mine.

Ms. Kelly went on to say that it would be marvelous if I made something for show and tell. My mom also thought that idea was marvelous. The worried expression on my mom's face and Ms. Kelly's big smile let me know that this was going to be a mandatory thing. With no way out, I told them I would bring in an ant farm. I figured an ant farm would be something I could put together quickly without spending any money. So early in the morning, before any normal person had thoughts of getting up, I was walking on the embankment of the irrigation canal that ran alongside my school, crossing the small wooden bridge that went over it, and entering the schoolyard. I headed toward the sandy area at the end of the playground and passed the big, dilapidated slide--once the most awesome thing in the playground, now an old eyesore, its function reduced to being the object of double dares. Anyone who took the dare and slid down that rusted thing ran the risk of falling off or at the very least, ripping off an important piece of clothing. I was not a risk taker. I never chanced it no matter what kids called me.

I made my way behind a cluster of mulberry trees and stopped in front of an anthill. After a quick look, I figured that one ant was as good as any other. I placed the ginger ale bottle beside me and took out a kitchen spoon from my back pocket. After spooning some sand into the bottle, I reached for an ant. For some reason, though, another ant caught my eye at that moment. It didn't look any different from the one I was reaching for except that it was struggling with a breadcrumb that was lodged between two pebbles. Curious, I pushed the pebbles aside with my finger and waited to see what the ant would do. When the ant didn't move, I prodded it. The ant hurried away from me, but not before grabbing the breadcrumb with its mandibles.

"Hey! Don't go anywhere! You, little ant, will be the keeper of my ant farm," I said.

Chasing the ant with my spoon, I scooped it up along with the breadcrumb and dropped both inside the bottle. I reached into the folds of my left sock and pulled out a sugar cube. I had found the sugar cube under Ms. Kelly's desk during one of my snooping expeditions. It had been in the farthest corner, the part the janitor had ignored for weeks. What the sugar cube was doing there, I had no idea, but I snatched it up thinking I would find a use for it sooner or later.

"Here you go," I said, dropping the sugar cube into the bottle.

From a distance, the morning bell buzzed. I snatched up my bottle and ran inside into room

106. I was nervous walking into the classroom with the bottle, now officially my ant farm.

Everyone gathered around me and peered into it as soon as I walked in. I was the center of attention for once, a situation that never happened to me before, and found myself enjoying it. I was discussing my ant farm with the others when Marcella Archuleta, who everyone called Marcie, walked into the room.

"What's that?" asked Marcie. Not waiting for an answer, she tossed back her curly, brown hair. There was a hint of a smile when she saw the look of panic on my face. "Ms. Kelly! Joseph has a dirty bottle on his desk, and it's full of bugs!"

"It's not full of bugs. It's one ant. One little ant and the bottle isn't dirty. I cleaned it last night... with soap." Nothing I said made a difference to Marcie. I began to regret the ant farm idea and tried to hide it under my desk before Ms. Kelly got to us, but I was not fast enough.

"Good morning, everyone," greeted Ms. Kelly.

"Ms. Kelly, look at that dirty bottle. There are bugs inside it. Remember, I'm allergic to dirt and bugs. I'm not supposed to be near that stuff. I could get sick. I mean really, really sick," complained Marcie. To prove how sensitive her health was, she let out a few hacking coughs.

I wanted to give Marcie a dirty look to let her know that I knew she was lying, but I kept my head down. I wanted to forget the whole ant farm thing. I decided then that I didn't need to get out of my comfort zone. I was ... well comfortable with the way things were. Being ignored. No eyes on me.

This was torture.

Ms. Kelly looked down at my ant farm bottle and asked, "Joseph, is this your project?"

"Project?" I wanted to correct Ms. Kelly. The ant farm was a show and tell thing not a project, but Ms. Kelly was already announcing to everyone that I had a treat for them.

Ms. Kelly clapped her hands to get everyone's attention and said, "Joseph has put together a wonderful presentation!"

At the word presentation, blood rushed to

my head and my knees began shaking. In less than a second, my show and tell thing grew into a project and then mushroomed into a presentation! A presentation was a lot harder than a show-and-tell thing. I wiped the sweat off my forehead and cleared my throat.

"Ms. Kelly, it's nothing," I stammered. "It's an old bottle with one ant."

"Why don't you begin with an explanation on what your presentation is all about?" suggested Ms. Kelly as she waved me to the front of the class with an encouraging smile. At that moment, there was nothing I could do but take my place at the front of the class holding the soda bottle--my ant farm, whatever. My heart pounded as I faced everyone, and an eerie silence filled the room.

"Joseph, tell us about your bottle," prompted Ms. Kelly.

"The bottle is full of dirt," Marcie began before I could open my mouth.

Ms. Kelly shook her head. Marcie folded her arms and waited with the others. With my head down to avoid eye contact, I mumbled something about the anthill, the ant, and the sugar cube. Everyone started to complain that they couldn't hear me.

"Joseph, a little louder. You need to speak clearly and project your voice out, so you can be heard," advised Ms. Kelly.

My whole body went numb. I nodded,

pretending I knew what Ms. Kelly meant. I continued. I didn't know if I was yelling or whispering the words. All I knew was that my lips were moving. At one point, my voice cracked and squeaked. I heard someone ask Ms. Kelly if I was crying. My hands shook as I raised my ant farm to show everyone. That's all I can remember. The rest was a blur.

"Ms. Kelly, there is only one ant in there," Marcie interrupted, not even bothering to raise her hand. "You can't have an ant farm with only one. The ones they sell in the stores have a bunch of ants and you can see the ant tunnels. And another thing, that bottle is green. It's hard to see the ant. AND another thing, he got the bottle from the trash."

It was a miracle that I stayed standing after that. Who wouldn't want one of those fancy ant farms where you could see all the ants and their tunnels? I didn't want to explain to everyone that I did not have money to buy one from the store.

"Well, how many ants does one need?" Ms. Kelly asked. "I think this one ant is perfect for this ant farm. This is a terrific idea. Not only did Joseph make an ant farm on his own, but he is helping the environment by recycling. Very clever, Joseph." Ms. Kelly walked over to me and peered into my green bottle. "What a magnificent ant. Bravo, Joseph!"

"Thanks," I mumbled. I continued standing,

not sure what I was supposed to do next. Was I supposed to bow to show that I was done? A smirk on Marcie's face jolted me out of my frozen state, moving me fast down the aisle to the safety of my desk.

"Joseph, why don't you set up your ant farm on one of the desks in the back? Don't forget to cover the top of the bottle so you won't lose your ant," said Ms. Kelly.

My hands were still shaking as I placed my ant farm on an empty desk. I tore off a piece of paper and reached to my belt where I had a supply of twisty ties on a belt loop. Using a twisty tie to hold the paper in place over the opening of the bottle, I poked a few small holes through the paper.

"That was bad," I whispered to the ant, who was furiously waving his antennae. "That stinky Marcie. She thinks she is the boss of everyone. Well, I'm not doing that again. I don't need to interact with my class. I don't have a problem."

I tapped the bottle to get the ant's attention. "But you did good, little ant. For doing such a good job, as soon as I can, I'll take you back home. I promise. I cross my heart, pinky swear, and all that stuff. Don't move. I'll be right back."

Chapter 2

The Metamorphosis

WATCHING THE HUMAN WALK AWAY, the ant was worried. Before he found himself in this place, he remembered that he had been foraging for food a few feet north of the hill. Without warning, he found himself rising and plummeting into a dark cavern. Moments later, the ant's world began to shake and swing. He looked up and was startled to see a human. The human was a medium size boy with dark eyes and short brown hair. Everything the boy was wearing was either too big for him or too tight. On his feet were a pair of dirty and torn shoes with a big toe protruding from one shoe.

Without warning, the movements had stopped. The ant remembered looking up to find more human faces staring down at him. His antennae waved wildly as he tried to send a signal to other ants that he was in danger.

He shut his eyes and braced for some form of attack, but nothing happened.

"I think he's dead," said a voice.

"Naw. He's just scared," answered the boy who had been carrying the ant. He tapped the bottle. "See, it's moving now."

The ant opened his eyes. Still furiously waving his antennae, he stared up at the humans as they stared back.

"He's looking at me," said one of the humans.

"No, he's looking at me," another one argued.

After a while, they all went away except for the boy who carried him to this place. The ant listened to the boy's words. The words, "I'll be right back" echoed in the bottle as the boy walked away.

Now, he was all alone. Intending to just stay still and wait for the boy's return, the ant changed his mind when he felt a rumbling in his belly. The ant's antennae detected something inside his small prison. He used his tiny claws at the end of his feet to sift through the sand. He found a white object and took a nibble. It was sweet. Normally, he would have carried any find back to the hill for distribution and storage, but his current situation made him feel like he could make an exception this one time. He ate it. The sweet treat calmed the rumbling in his stomach.

He decided he would not bother the boy and would try to find his own way out. He trudged through the sand looking for an opening. Feeling a heaviness in his feet, he looked down and found his feet encrusted with gooey stuff, a mixture of the sugary treat and sand. Using his antenna, he scraped off the unwanted stuff from his feet only to relocate it onto his antenna. He placed his sticky feet on the wall of his plastic prison and slapped his antenna with full force against it. The impact caused the sand to fly off his antenna and firmly glue his feet to the wall. He was stuck!

Defeated, the ant dangled while he contemplated his next move. He could not stay hanging forever. He had to keep fighting. After a good amount of kicking and twisting, the ant freed himself. There was still enough sticky stuff on his feet to keep him secure on the wall of his prison, so he decided to try to crawl up the bottle. After a bit of effort, he managed to squeeze himself through one of the holes at the top. He was free!

The ant headed toward the closet door, detecting a smell. It was the scent of food, lots of food. He followed the scent into the closet, filled with jackets, backpacks, and lunchboxes. He squeezed inside the nearest lunchbox and found a sandwich along with a box of juice. He ate the sandwich and drank the juice. He continued to explore every lunchbox and gobbled down everything he found, including a fish burrito, which he didn't find that appetizing at all. By the time he finished with the last lunchbox, he barely managed to squeeze his swollen belly out and slumped to the floor. Heavy-eyed and sluggish, he crawled under a jacket he found on the floor and drifted off to sleep.

For the first time in his life, the ant found himself dreaming. The dream began pleasant enough. There was a door that led to a room, with tables that towered with desserts. He ran into the room and gorged on it all--chocolate cake, strawberry shortcake with mountains of whipped cream, a tripled pineapple upside down cake...sometime between the whipped cream and the pineapple upside down cake, his tummy began to hurt. A cake, with curly brown smoke radiating from it, came out of the shadows screaming at him in a high pitched, piercing voice. He tried to appease it

by offering it some whipped cream. The raging cake wagged its finger at him, flickering whipped cream back at him as it slowly approached. Frightened, he ran away but tripped over his own legs. He felt himself falling. His body twitched, and his legs jerked about wildly. He abruptly awoke and found not a rampaging cake, but a human with a head of curly hair in front of him.

"You're on my jacket!" she yelled in the same shrill voice of his dream. He covered his face with jackets and hoped the human would go away.

"Are you deaf? I said you're on my jacket!" When the pile of jackets remained still, the human stomped her foot. "You're in big trouble, mister. Ms. Kelly! There's...uh...there's a funny looking kid sleeping on all our jackets. He's messing up our stuff."

"What is it, Marcie?" Ms. Kelly asked when she looked in.

"He's in there," said Marcie and pointed to the jackets.

The ant uncovered a small portion of his face to see who the curly haired girl had called to her side. A tall, thin human with yellow hair towered over him.

"My goodness. Who are you?" she asked.

"I think we should call the police," insisted Marcie. "He doesn't look safe."

The ant stared in silence. He looked toward

the door looking to escape only to find it blocked by a crowd of humans, the very same ones that had been staring at him through the bottle earlier that morning.

"Are you a new student?" asked Ms. Kelly, receiving a blank stare as a response to her question.

"Maybe he doesn't speak English," suggested Marcie. "You want me to ask him in Spanish, Ms. Kelly?"

Marcie proceeded to question the boy in Spanish, "*¿Eres estudiante nuevo aqui*?" When the boy didn't answer, she reported to her teacher, "Nope. He doesn't speak Spanish."

"Who is it? What's he doing?" asked the other humans from the doorway.

"I'll tell you what he's doing. He's on my jacket and he's making it all wrinkly," complained Marcie. She pointed her finger at the boy. "He needs to buy me a new one."

"Marcie, that's enough," said Ms. Kelly and turned to her students. "Let's all wait in our seats to meet the newest member to our class. And yes Marcie, that includes you."

Marcie frowned. Ms. Kelly turned back to the boy hidden in the jackets. "We'll give you a moment to regroup before you join us."

Before leaving the doorway, each student gave one last glance at the new kid. Last in line was a human who the ant instantly recognized. It was the boy who promised to take him back to the hill! This was his chance! The ant struggled to get out of the jackets as the boy turned to leave, hoping to catch him before he did. The movement caused the boy to stop and turn around.

Chapter 3
The New Kid

I PAUSED WHEN I SAW THE new kid try to stand up. The darkness in the closet made it difficult for me to see. At first, when my eyes adjusted, all I saw were jackets. Then, my eyes found the new kid's face.

For once, Marcie had not been exaggerating. He *was* funny looking. He had a reddish-brown face with a huge pair of black eyes, smooth round cheeks, a powerful looking jaw, and a little nothing of a nose. I stayed at the doorway watching the kid try to get up.

As the jackets fell away, I got a little scared. I couldn't help it. Under all the jackets, the kid was completely naked. He was shorter than me with a whole lot of skinny all over him. He had long skinny arms, long skinny fingers, and skinny legs with abnormally long skinny toes. When the last jacket that laid on his head fell away, I lost it and screamed, a loud squeaky kind of scream. On the kid's head were two long... wriggly things!

"What are...those?" I asked. My finger shook as I pointed to them.

After a minute of clearing his throat, the kid grumpily replied, "It's about time."

"What?" I stammered.

"You said you were coming right back. You promised," exclaimed the kid. He shook his head and waved his skinny arms. He was mad and clearly crazy. "Just carry me back now!"

"I'm not going to carry you anywhere. I don't know you," I told him. I crossed my arms, looked him over, and added, "You know, you do look familiar."

"Yeah. You saw me this morning," said the kid. He nervously looked around the closet. He stopped waving his arms and stared intently at me. "You said I did good, and punky shirt and stuff."

"I said *pinky swear* and," I paused and thought for a second. I asked, "Hey, how do you know what I said to my ant?"

The kid jumped up and down. I shook my head and insisted, "You weren't there."

"You were there," said the kid as he jabbed me on the chest. Then, he pointed to himself and added, "and me, the ant, was there."

"You're saying," I jabbed him right back on the chest just like he did to me, "that you're my ant?"

I had to be on one of those television shows that do jokes on people. What else could this be? Worried about ending up on television with a naked kid, I leaned close to him and whispered, “You should put your clothes back on. Where’s the camera?”

Before I could move away, the kid leaned his head back and let out a moan filled with fear and desperation which just about caused me to fall over in a dead faint. I started to panic.

“You sick or something? Do you want me to get Ms. Kelly’s phone so you can call your mom?” I asked.

The kid gave me a look as if I was the one who was crazy. He let out another moan and began pounding his head on the wall. I stood paralyzed, not knowing what to do. My eyes kept moving up to the things on the kid’s head, which never stopped wriggling.

I pointed to his head and asked, “How do you get those things to wriggle? Are they battery operated?”

My questions were ignored. He kept pounding his head. It occurred to me that maybe the kid honestly believed he was an ant. So, I asked him, “Hey, aren’t you supposed to have six legs? If you’re an ant, why are you able to talk? Huh?”

The pounding stopped. Next thing I knew, we were standing toe to toe, face to face, both of us studying the other. Staring into his face was like staring into one of those 3D pictures that you need to focus at a certain angle to see the hidden image. With my close angle, the hidden image in the kid's face emerged. I was staring into the face of an ant!

"I ... I," I struggled to get words out of my mouth. All those spooky stories that I grew up with swirled in my head. Could this ant thing be *El Cucuy*? I knew it wasn't *La Llorona* because that monster was a lady. I took a deep breath to calm myself, but a voice behind me jolted me back into panic mode. I whirled around thinking I was going to find a vampire or zombie standing there to eat my flesh (because why would I expect anything less at this point?), only to find Irwin De La Rosa.

"Ms. Kelly and Marcie want to know what's all that banging noise. And why it's taking so long for you guys to come out?" asked Irwin. He adjusted his glasses and peered through his thick lenses at me. "Was that you who screamed? What's wrong?"

"Yeah. I saw a...there was a...I saw a bug," I squeaked.

"You did? What type of bug?" Interested, Irwin took a step inside the closet, but I blocked him.

"It was a...cockroach," I lied. Scared as I was, I wasn't ready to tell anyone what I discovered, especially to Irwin. He was easily the smartest kid in school. He had one of those brains that was loaded with smart stuff and was constantly sharing it with the rest of us, like it or not. This habit made him annoying--and I had a habit of not trusting annoying people.

"Really? You know they're absolutely harmless," said Irwin.

"Not this one. This one's big, really big," I told Irwin. He leaned in to get a look at the cockroach. Again, I blocked him.

"Come on, let me see it," pleaded Irwin. "Did you know that the biggest cockroach on record is the Megaloblatta cockroach from Peru? It can grow to be almost four inches long, and it can fly. Then, there's the Australian giant burrowing cockroach. That one can grow to be three and a half inches long. That one is considered to be the heaviest cockroach. Then there's the Madagascar hissing cockroach which is the creepiest because it hisses. Now that one can grow to be three inches long. How big is this one?"

"Listen, Irwin, do me a favor and go check on my ant," I said. I was hoping my ant was still in the ginger ale bottle, and this was just one funny looking kid.

"Okay," said Irwin.

I closed the door and leaned my ear against it to listen. Curious, the ant leaned his ear on the door and listened along with me. In no time, we heard a light tap. Irwin had returned.

"Sorry, Joseph. It's not in the bottle. It must have escaped," replied Irwin through the closed door.

"Rats!" It was not what I wanted to hear. "Listen, Irwin, I have to keep the door closed so the thing won't escape. Don't tell Ms. Kelly that there's a bug in here. Just tell her we will be out soon."

It was a known fact that Ms. Kelly was deathly afraid of bugs. It did not matter if it was a fuzzy, friendly caterpillar or a creepy spider. No one could forget the day when a grasshopper made its way into the classroom, and Ms. Kelly lost it. I mean, she freaked out. She jumped up on a desk and screamed that we needed to smash the innocent grasshopper to bits and throw it into the trash bin located far outside near the parking lot. For being in her twenties, she moved fast. I didn't think old people could move that fast or jump that high.

"All right," agreed Irwin. He did not have to be reminded. "Joseph, don't kill the cockroach, but if you do, save it for me. And if you don't, still save it for me. Okay?"

"Yeah, yeah," I said. I pressed my ear against the door and listened as Irwin told Ms. Kelly that we would be out soon. I turned and looked at the ant in silence. I should have run out of the closet screaming for help, but I didn't. Not once in the whole time I had been going to school had I ever made a commotion.

I was not a drama type of kid. If this kid was the ant I caught, put in a bottle, and brought here, I was in a hot mess! I needed time to figure things out. Whatever I decided had to be simple, with no risk of drama.

"Um. First, please don't eat me. Second, sorry for the bottle thing." I said. I kept a close eye on the ant looking for any signs of attack. I was so sure he was going to suck my blood like a vampire or something crazy like that, but all I saw was sadness on the ant's face. I reached out and gave him a soft pat on his shoulder. "I never was going to hurt you. I don't hurt living things. Honest. I put a sugar cube in the bottle for you."

The ant began to gag and cough. I stepped away. He spat into his hand. He pushed his hand up to my face and asked, "Want it back?"

I peered into the palm of his hand and saw some white mucus gunk. Gross! It was all that was left of the sugar cube. Feeling queasy, I gagged and grunted out, "No thanks. You can keep it." The ant smiled and slurped up the sugary mess. A feeling of dread washed over me as I realized that on the other side of the closet door was a classroom full of third graders eager to meet this ant-kid. Sneaking this overgrown ant out of the building and back to the anthill was going to be impossible during the day.

"Can you get small again?" I whispered. "It

would really help me out. If you get small, I can put you in my pocket."

"Don't know how," he said with a shrug.

"Maybe you just need to think small. Close your eyes and think small. Got it?" I instructed. The ant nodded and did what I told him to do. Nothing happened.

"Are you trying hard? You need to think hard," I said.

He insisted that he was. I looked for any signs of shrinking, but all I saw was the ant's face turning from reddish brown to a purplish color. He looked just like I did that time I ate a pound of cheese and spent the whole day in the bathroom. I motioned him to stop. Disappointed, we both sat down and leaned against the wall.

"Everything is so messed up," I sighed. Then, an idea came to me. "You have to go out there. They're waiting to meet a new kid. We need to make that happen."

The ant shook his head. I continued, "I know it's scary for you, but it's the best way for me to get you out of here. Of course, we will need to camouflage you before walking out. Maybe you need to wear out the bigness that happened to you to get small again. When you do, I can return you to the anthill."

The ant still was not convinced.

"If they see you like this, they'll go crazy and not in a good way," I said. I did not mention the oversized can of bug spray Ms. Kelly had in her desk, bottom left-hand side, ready for use at any sign of insect infestation. I leaned closer to the ant and whispered, "Someone might call the government."

This situation was sort of like a book I read about an alien that was left behind on Earth. The government wanted the alien to conduct experiments on it. If the government found out about this ant, they would be breaking down the school doors in a second.

"The government would love to have you," I began. The ant smiled, but the smile changed into a look of terror when I finished with, "to chop you up and put your body pieces into a jar so they could do experiments."

That did it. The ant was willing to leave the closet under my terms. The first thing I did was find clothes for him, which was easy. There were always forgotten clothes stuffed in the upper shelves of the closet. In no time, I found a long sleeve blue shirt, white socks, and a pair of high-top tennis shoes. Lucky for us, I discovered a black baseball cap wedged deep in the shelves. The cap was the perfect thing to hide the wriggly antennae. We had everything except for pants.

Then, I had an idea. I fished out a pair of jeans tucked away in a box marked "Ezequiel's Extra". The pants belonged to Ezequiel Montez, who had what Ms. Kelly called a "sensitive nerve problem”. It was Ms. Kelly’s polite way of saying that Ezequiel had a bathroom problem. Stressful situations caused Ezequiel to wet his pants, or as Ms. Kelly called it, “little accidents”. It had been happening since kindergarten, so we were used to it. I hated using the “little accident” pants, but I was desperate. I got the pants out of the box and handed them to the ant. The ant looked like a boy once he was dressed, but he didn’t look pleased.

“What’s wrong?” I asked.

“I don’t look like you,” he complained and pointed to my shoe with my big toe sticking out of the big hole. “Mine don’t do that.”

"Your toes are not supposed to show," I said trying not to show my embarrassment. Both my shoe and my hand-me-down sock had large holes where my big toe was. I squatted down, took off my shoe, and rearranged the sock so my toe would be covered. I showed the ant my covered toe. "That's the right way. Say...what should we call you?"

"Call me, Say," he said.

"Say is not a name. It's just a word," I explained. "What about Seymour?"

"I like that. Call me, Saygar."

"I said Seymour, not Saygar," I corrected. I was going to explain the difference, but the ant crossed his arms and pouted. I had no idea that ants could be stubborn. "All right. Your name is Saygar."

Chapter 4

Pretty Little Ears

ALL EYES WERE ON US when I opened the door. Just like in my presentation, I got the jittery shakes as we walked out of the closet. My heart began pounding and my hands were slimy with sweat. Once again, an eerie silence filled the classroom. I took a deep breath and motioned Saygar to follow me. As soon as Saygar took his first step, I saw trouble: he was not used to wearing shoes or having only two legs, so he was struggling to stay upright. He swayed and stumbled down the aisle, swinging his arms to balance himself. In the process, he managed to swipe books off desks and slap a few students on their heads as he wobbled his way to the front of the classroom.

Marcie leaned dangerously out of her chair to get a better look at Saygar. The way she was looking at him worried me. If anyone would see pass Saygar's disguise, it would be Marcie. After what seemed like hours, Saygar made it to the front and stood beside me.

"It's about time," exclaimed Marcie, breaking the silence. Ms. Kelly shot her a disapproving look, and Marcie shrugged. "Well, he took forever."

I held my breath. This was the moment of truth. Was Ms. Kelly going to scream out for the bug spray or was she going to welcome Saygar? I was ready to yell for Saygar to make a run for it when Ms. Kelly smiled.

"Good morning," Ms. Kelly said to Saygar. "Class, what do we say?"

"Good morning! Welcome to our class," we recited.

"Why don't you tell us your name?" asked Ms. Kelly. Saygar shifted nervously and cleared his throat but did not say a word.

"Ms. Kelly, his name is Saygar A. Hill," I smoothly answered. I was proud of myself for thinking of the middle initial, I thought it was a good touch. I couldn't believe how easy I lied. I am not a good liar--my red face, twitching eyes, and stammering usually give me away.

"Well, Saygar, tell us something about yourself," said Ms. Kelly.

"He's from Indiana," I answered. I don't know why I picked that state except that it sounded like a place far away from El Paso.

"You are!" exclaimed Ms. Kelly. Her eyes widen with interest. "I'm also from Indiana."

Oops, I thought. I changed Indiana to Alaska. I was surprised at how quickly the lies were flowing out of my mouth.

"How lovely! Tell us all about Alaska," said Ms. Kelly.

Saygar had finally found his voice. "I used to live out there," he began and pointed to the window. Everyone shifted in their seats to get a look at the window. Then, Saygar pointed to me and finished with, "He carried me into this room, put some clothes on me in that room over there, and now I'm here."

For a second, I actually stopped breathing. I stared at the ceiling to avoid any eye contact. I listened to the sounds of my classmates twisting in their chairs to look in my direction. Feeling their stares on me, I felt my eye-twitching thing starting up.

"What!" gasped Marcie.

"It looks like we have a comedian in our classroom," laughed Ms. Kelly. "We are happy to have you, Saygar A. Hill from Alaska. We hope you like it here. Joseph, why don't you be Saygar's buddy this week and help him figure out his way around the school?"

I ushered Saygar to the back of the room, to the desk behind Arianna Bustamante, the shyest girl in the class, and across from my own. I sat down and relaxed for the first time that morning. I just had to keep an eye on Saygar a little while longer until the perfect time came to return him to where he belonged. In the meantime, we would have to sit still for Ms. Kelly's math lesson.

Saygar tried to blend in, doing what we were doing. He stared at the pages of his math book, watched Ms. Kelly write squiggly lines on the board, and listened to her go on about numbers and sums. Being an ant who was usually quite busy, he found it hard to sit still. It didn't take long for Saygar to get antsy. I'm not an ant, but I couldn't blame him for having trouble. There were times after sitting for a long time in class when I thought I might do something crazy, like jumping up and down or yelling something dumb like "Marcie has a turtle face" (even though she doesn't).

I think Saygar could have behaved a little longer if Ms. Kelly had not been up there at the board. It was that part, the listening part, that may have been where everything started going wrong. Everyone knows that when Ms. Kelly is up at the front writing on the board with her back to us, her voice changes. It becomes low and soft. It can put you to sleep if you're not careful. There was a way to listen to Ms. Kelly during those times. You had to lean forward in your seat as much as you can, not take deep breaths, sneeze, or cough. If you can manage it, don't breathe at all. If you don't do those things, you won't hear much.

Saygar didn't know the secrets of Ms. Kelly at the board. He listened, but all he got was the soft mumbling. Her low voice was a lullaby to him. I was not surprised when I saw him yawning. He rubbed his eyes and looked my way. I could barely see his eyes through his droopy eyelids. I nudged him awake.

"Pay attention to Ms. Kelly," I whispered and opened his math book to the correct page.

I watched Saygar keep his eyes on Ms. Kelly until he went cross-eyed. I'm pretty sure by that time, Saygar found Ms. Kelly at the board boring. He began looking around for something more interesting. His eyes zeroed in on Arianna. He probably had never been this close to a human head before. I could see him studying her. Her long brown hair was pulled neatly into a ponytail and gave Saygar a clear view of her slightly large ears. He leaned closer to one ear and slowly moved over to the other. He signaled for me to look at her ear and pointed to the small golden ring dangling from it.

I shook my head and insisted, "Watch Ms. Kelly."

He did a quick glance around the room to make sure he was not being watched. Feeling that the coast was clear, he inched his knees up on the seat of his chair and slowly maneuvered himself on his desktop. I cleared my throat trying to get his attention. He ignored me. He got as close as he could get to Arianna's ears and continued to stare. Saygar was so close to Arianna that when I saw her frown, I knew she could feel his presence. Puzzled, she turned slightly to see what it was, jumping a little when she found herself face to face with Saygar. She leaned away from him, but he moved with her. Not wanting to make a scene, she ignored him, probably praying he would go away. She stared straight ahead not daring to breathe or even blink. When it became clear to her that Saygar wasn't going away, she raised her hand to get Ms. Kelly's attention.

"Get down," I hissed to Saygar.

Marcie was doing her usual visual patrol looking for any signs of trouble, so she could be the one to tell Ms. Kelly. I saw her look in our direction. She did a double take. I saw her dramatically mouth, "Oh my gosh". It was as clear as if she had yelled out the words. Marcie didn't even wait to raise her hand, just yelling out, "Oh, Ms. Kelly!"

"Wait a minute, Marcie," answered Ms. Kelly, continuing to write on the board and keeping her back to the class.

"Ms. Kelly," whimpered Arianna. Her raised hand trembled.

"Get down, Saygar," I commanded. He paid absolutely no attention to me. He remained on the desk staring at Arianna. I grabbed at him but missed. I looked over at Marcie and our eyes met. Her cold stare made it clear to me that she was about to tell Ms. Kelly. Desperately trying to get Saygar down before then, I made another attempt at grabbing him. I lurched clumsily in Saygar's direction and fell over into the aisle. As I hit the floor, I heard Arianna scream. At the same time, Marcie made her move.

"*Ms. Kelly*!" Marcie's loud, demanding voice thundered and vibrated through the room. Everyone jumped in their seats as Ms. Kelly whirled around.

"My goodness. Marcie, inside voice, please," scolded Ms. Kelly.

With all eyes on Marcie, she waved her arms and in a dramatic gesture pointed both hands at Saygar who had remained perched on the desktop. She shouted, "The kid from Alaska is trying to bite Arianna's ears!"

Feeling more confident after Marcie's weird arm waving outburst, Arianna was brave enough to scream out, "He's trying to eat my ears!"

All the screaming and hand pointing confused Saygar and caused him to lose his balance and topple off his desk. I thought it was as good of a time as ever to try to get him back to the hill. I crawled toward Saygar but stopped as I felt a wave of pain start through my head and move through the rest of my body. I closed my eyes for a second. When I opened them, Irwin was in front of me.

"Ouch!" I cried and rubbed my head.

"Where is it?" asked Irwin.

Confused, I shrugged my shoulders and asked, "What are you talking about?"

"Saygar found the cockroach on Arianna," Irwin whispered and looked around. "That's what you're looking for, right?"

I was about to tell Irwin how crazy he was when an idea came to me. I said, "Yeah! Saygar heard an ugly hissing sound and saw it crawling on Arianna. He tried to grab it, but that thing was so big that it karate chopped Saygar's hand away and escaped."

Irwin's mouth dropped open and exclaimed, "That's so cool! Which way did it go?"

"Over there," I told Irwin. I pointed to the farthest corner of the room to divert his attention away from Saygar. I hurried past him, and when I reached Saygar, I helped him up. I told him not to say a word. By this time, the room was in total chaos, and Ms. Kelly was doing the usual stuff to try and quiet everyone. She raised her hand which was her signal to stop talking but no one stopped. She clapped her hands. It was ignored. She ended up screaming for all of us to be quiet. No one heard her.

"There's a giant cockroach running around the room! I'm positive it is a Madagascar

hissing cockroach which could easily be over three inches long. Don't worry, Ms. Kelly. Joseph, Saygar, and I are going to find it," Irwin announced. His voice cut through the commotion, and the news of a three-inch-long hissing cockroach running loose in the room had a quieting effect on everyone.

"Let's all return to our desks," gasped Ms. Kelly, speaking in a hushed voice as if the cockroach might be listening. She tiptoed to her desk and pulled out her bug spray. Everyone followed her example and tiptoed back to their seats, quietly waiting. Ms. Kelly gave the bug spray a firm shake and saturated the perimeter of her desk. She barely managed to choke out the words, "Does anyone see it?"

"Don't worry, Ms. Kelly. You'll probably hear it before you see it. It's a hissing cockroach.

It sounds something like this," Irwin took a deep breath, tightened his lips, and mimicked the hissing of the Madagascar cockroach. "Ssssssh ... Hisssss ... Ssssssh."

The blood drained from Ms. Kelly's face leaving her white as a ghost.

"Ms. Kelly, what about Saygar?" asked Marcie. I held my breath as I waited for Ms. Kelly's answer. Cradling the bug spray can in her arms, she stared at Marcie, that weird kind of stare where a person is looking at you, but not actually *seeing* you. Marcie repeated her question but got no answer. It was obvious to me that Ms. Kelly was in no condition to deal with the Saygar and Arianna situation. Feeling relief that Ms. Kelly's bug problem turned her into a zombie (and feeling a bit guilty about it), I walked away to help search for the nonexistent cockroach.

Chapter 5

Burps and Farts

I LEARNED MY LESSON AFTER THE Arianna incident: I had to keep Saygar busy and out of trouble. The hissing cockroach ruckus left everyone looking over their shoulders and staying away from dark places in the classroom. Everyone was worried that they would be the one to find the hissing monster. My worry was that they would figure out that there was no such thing. Ms. Kelly gave the order that at any sign of the hissing beast, whether visual or audio, we were to grab the bug spray and drown it with the poison.

Despite her paralyzing fears, Ms. Kelly tried her best to get her class back to normal. She went back to teaching, and we went back to learning. Ms. Kelly had moved Saygar from the desk behind Arianna to a desk behind Ruby Rubio, an aisle away from me, which made it harder for me to watch him. I got out my box of crayons and some paper for Saygar, so he could color. He seemed content drawing and sneaking bites off the crayons.

But any movement or a hint of a whisper of an odd sound had everyone jumping in their seats with Ms. Kelly hollering, "What's that?"

Exhausted and ready for a break, I was relieved when Ms. Kelly announced it was time for lunch. We got our lunchboxes from the closet and marched to the cafeteria. When we sat down to eat, we were all surprised to find every single lunchbox empty.

"Someone stole all our lunches!" complained Jorge Antonio Gonzales Jr., or as he was known, Georgie Jr.. Georgie Jr.'s mother always packed two lunchboxes for him, one for his actual lunch and one just for his Twinkies. Both were empty.

Ms. Kelly was just as surprised. There was nothing she could do except lead us to the cafeteria line for a tray of spaghetti and meatballs, a fruit cup, and some chocolate pudding. While we used our forks to eat, Saygar crammed a handful of spaghetti noodles into his mouth. He smacked his lips noisily, chewing with his mouth open.

"Close your mouth," scolded Marcie. She sat across from him and had a close-up view of the food rolling around in his mouth. I whispered to Saygar, who sat next to me, to drink his milk to wash down the food.

"I wonder what happened to our lunches?" asked Lorenzo Mora, who always over-moussed his black hair and combed it neatly to one side. Ms. Kelly once said he looked just like Elvis.

"It's weird that all of our lunches disappeared at the same time," said Irwin. He stopped to watch Saygar cram another fistful of noodles into his mouth. "Since I didn't see any strangers this morning, I have concluded that it was an inside job."

Georgie Jr. pointed to Saygar and muttered, "Maybe not a stranger, but there was someone strange in the closet. It was that guy."

"You're right. Hey, Saygar, did you see anything suspicious?" asked Irwin. His eyes widened as he realized that there could be a witness to the lunchbox heist. Saygar shook his head and burped. He poured his pudding over his spaghetti and stirred it with a spoon. Irwin rubbed his chin as he thought. He looked around at the rest of us and said, "It probably was that cockroach. Those hissing cockroaches have ferocious appetites."

Saygar let out another burp. Worried that the food was giving Saygar the burps, I urged him to drink more milk, which he did. He added his fruit to the spaghetti and pudding mixture, leaned over his tray, and slurped it all up. To wash it down, he took a drink from his milk carton. He gagged and spit out all that was in his mouth back onto his tray.

"Eww! You're so gross," complained Marcie. "You're not supposed to do that at the table."

"Saygar, what are you doing?" I asked. I shifted nervously, getting a jittery feeling in the pit of my stomach.

"Want some?" offered Saygar. I shook my head. Without any warning, another burp thundered out of Saygar.

"Whoa, that was loud," laughed Lorenzo.

It occurred to me that the burps were getting louder and coming out faster. As I sat thinking about the burps and what they meant, Saygar slurped the mess of food from his tray back into his mouth. His cheeks puffed out. I could see that he was trying to swallow but couldn't.

"Saygar, just spit it out. You don't need to eat it," I told him.

"He better not spit. That's what he gets for making a mess with his spaghetti," said Marcie. She pointed her finger at Saygar and gave him a direct order. "You eat it."

It was plain to me that Saygar wanted to spit, but with Marcie sitting in front of him giving him mean looks, he didn't dare. He took a deep breath and swallowed, managing to force some of the food down his throat. In the middle of the usual cafeteria clamor, the distinct sound of digestive noises could be heard. Startled, everyone at the table stopped what they were doing and glanced around, their eyes landing on Saygar. Saygar clutched at his stomach, and a low-pitch rumble came out of him.

"The new kid just tooted," I heard someone say.

"I smell it," Marcie cried out. She pinched her nose and waved the smell away from her.

Another rumble was released, louder than the first. Saygar jumped and looked under his seat to look for the source of the noises. I was in a panic. This ant situation had turned serious. Saygar was about to be labeled "the kid who rips them in the cafeteria."

"Saygar, stop that," I urged.

Saygar wrapped his arms around his twitching stomach and put all his weight on his bottom. There was a determined expression on his face as he attempted to squish the rumbles away. For a moment, there was silence. Just when I thought the coast was clear, a series of short, high-pitched ripples blasted out of Saygar. All of us, including Saygar, covered our noses.

"Stink bomb!" gasped Lorenzo.

"Oh my gosh!" choked Marcie.

"Kind of makes your eyes water, huh?" gagged Irwin.

"Are you all right, Saygar?" I wheezed. Saygar was not looking so good. He was white in the face.

"I think he's choking," said Irwin. "Does

anyone know how to do the Heimlich Maneuver?"

No one had heard of the Heimlich Maneuver.

I grabbed Saygar by the shoulders and begged, "Just spit."

"He better not," threatened Marcie.

"You're not the boss of him! He can spit if he wants," I snapped back.

"If he does, I'm telling Ms. Kelly about the mess and stuff that he's been doing," warned Marcie. She smiled and added, "I'll tell her that he was the one who stole our lunches."

"He better breathe soon," Irwin cut in. "Did you know that five minutes without oxygen could result in brain damage? That's all it takes, five little minutes."

"Spit!" I ordered. "Marcie, you better let him!"

While Marcie and I battled it out, Saygar was trying to rid himself of the mixture by forcing it down his throat with swallows. With each swallow, he gagged. He clutched his stomach bending over shivering and drooling.

"You guys, something is happening here," warned Irwin.

The arguing stopped. All eyes were on Saygar. It was not known whether Saygar was going to let out another stink bomb, throw up, or get brain damage. We just knew that all signs pointed to something big. He was red in the face, his nose twitched, and panic spread across his face. We held our breath and waited. When his food-packed face trembled, we knew. He was going to throw up.

"He's going to blow!" yelled Lorenzo.

We heeded Lorenzo's warning and jumped out of the line of fire. Every drop of spaghetti, pudding, fruit, and milk that had been in Saygar's body torpedoed out of his mouth and nose with a force that he probably had never felt before. I had to admit that it was a jaw-dropping moment. I had never seen anything like it. When it was all over, Saygar sighed with relief and looked around the table for something else to eat.

We had all moved out of the way just in time--except for Marcie. It was a shock to all of us to find her saturated with Saygar's lunch.

"She's going to rip me apart," I told myself. I braced myself for a whole lot of angry and rude words. To my disappointment, I heard sobs instead of insults. I saw tears instead of a chunk of my hair ripped off my head and in her hands. For the first time since I met her in kindergarten, I felt sorry for her. "Are you all right, Marcie?" I asked.

No one said a word as she wiped off her mouth and the area around her eyes. She got up and walked a few stiff steps away. She stopped and turned to face Saygar and me.

"You are so going to get it," she said through gritted teeth and marched away from the table.

I would have preferred she had punched me right then and there. The punch would have been over in a second. I mean how hard could she hit me? But a threat from Marcie was going to be around for a long time. I figured I was probably going to have to watch my back until middle school.

"That's a shame," sighed Irwin. "I bet Marcie wishes she had let Saygar spit." The others nodded in agreement.

Chapter 6

A New Home

AFTER LUNCH, I WATCHED MARCIE race over to Ms. Kelly waving her arms wildly to demonstrate what had just happened in the cafeteria. I was relieved to see that Marcie had cleaned up pretty good. Unfortunately, a strong whiff of Saygar's lunch mixture would escape from her hair every time she did the crazy arm waving thing. I hoped that Ms. Kelly had a weak sense of smell and not pick up on the stink. I stood next to Saygar and whispered to him not to say anything as Ms. Kelly approached.

"Saygar, did you spit up on Marcie?" asked Ms. Kelly.

"Yep," answered Saygar, ignoring what I had just told him.

"Ms. Kelly, he didn't mean to. I think he was choking," I said struggling to stay calm. "His eyes got all buggy, and he couldn't breathe! He almost got brain damage!"

"Ms. Kelly, he didn't spit. He threw up on me. He did it on purpose," Marcie interjected, poking out from behind Ms. Kelly. "He was making a mess when I told him to stop. He grabbed all this mess of food into his mouth and ... there was red stuff and brown pudding and noodles all over my face. I think some got in my mouth!" Marcie's voice trembled, and she paused to take a deep breath.

"Please don't cry," I prayed to myself. Nothing gets you into more trouble than having the person who is accusing you of something to be crying and smelly.

Irwin joined in, walking over to Saygar's other side. "He was choking, Ms. Kelly. It was necessary for him to vomit to avoid brain damage due to the lack of oxygen," he said. He gave Saygar a side glance and added, "He also suffered from an awful case of flatulence. Probably caused by his consumption of a dairy product. I mean milk. I think he's lactose intolerant."

"Ms. Kelly, he was burping and doing other awful stuff," complained Marcie. "It was stinky and gross!"

Everyone agreed, except for me. I refused to back up Marcie's story even though the stench caused by Saygar almost knocked me out.

I shrugged and said, "It wasn't that bad."

Ms. Kelly thought for a moment before saying, "I'm glad Saygar is fine. From this time on, it would be best to keep milk away from him. Saygar, we do not vomit on people at this school. Please, next time excuse yourself and go to the nurse's office or restroom."

"That's what I was saying!" exclaimed Marcie.

"Are you all right, Marcie?" asked Ms. Kelly.

"I guess," Marcie answered, giving Saygar a dirty look.

With a long sigh, Ms. Kelly said, "Let's line up so we can return to our classroom and get back to work."

The end of the day couldn't come fast enough. I was exhausted. When the bell rang, I snatched up my things, grabbed Saygar, and headed for home.

As we walked the streets, I realized that my day was not over. I had to find a place to stash Saygar where no one would notice him. I thought of hiding him under my bed but realized that wouldn't work. I shared my tiny room with my two older brothers, and they were ALWAYS in my business. I considered the laundry room but decided that wouldn't work either. I had a new baby sister and my mother was in that room washing the baby's things all the time.

I stopped in front of my home, a small white house with blue trim. It needed a paint job and maybe a new roof. It wasn't the prettiest house on the block, but it was home and I loved it anyway. I lifted the latch on the gate and entered the yard with Saygar following close behind me. We walked a pathway lined with my mother's blooming roses up to the front door.

"Have you ever been in a house?" I asked. Saygar shook his head. "Well it's not going to have tunnels like an anthill, so be prepared."

Saygar was silent as we walked into the house. The coast was clear: no one was in sight just yet.

"Mom, I'm home!" I yelled as we entered the living room. Not hearing a response, I knew that my mother was with my baby sister in the back bedroom. "Come on, Saygar. I'll make us dinner."

Once in the kitchen, I took out several eggs and scrambled them in a pan. I warmed two tortillas, placed some egg on them, and rolled them into burritos. I handed Saygar one as I took a bite of the other.

Saygar took a bite from his and frowned. He said, "Needs something."

"My mom puts chili in her burritos. Want some?" I asked. Saygar eagerly nodded. I pulled out a jelly jar which contained a mixture of jalapeno, onion, garlic, and tomato sauce. I added a spoonful of the chili to his burrito. As soon as he took a bite, I knew I was in trouble.

Saygar hopped around the kitchen spitting and coughing, flapping his arms like a dying bird!

"Hot?" I asked. Saygar's face was bright red. This wasn't good. Thinking fast, I decided that this was a mom emergency.

"MOM!" I shouted, hoping she was within hearing distance. "I gave my friend a lot of chili! What do I do?"

"Dairy products help calm down the heat!" my mom yelled back.

I searched the refrigerator for a dairy product. I knew milk was out of the question. So, I grabbed a stick of butter and handed it to Saygar. He didn't even bother to unwrap it before taking a bite and making a lot of noise as he chewed. All that smacking, and slurping made me wonder whether all ants had horrible eating habits or if it was just this one. The good thing was that the butter calmed down the heat in his mouth: his face returned to its usual brownish color.

"I don't have anything else to put in your burrito." I said. I peered into the refrigerator. "All I see is a bottle of syrup. That won't work cause it's sweet."

Saygar stood next to me and pointed to the syrup bottle. "I like sweet. I want the syrup."

"Yeah, I like syrup, but not in an egg burrito," I told him.

"I want it! I want it!" he insisted. I unrolled

his burrito, drizzled a good amount of syrup into it, and handed it back to him. He ate it in two bites. "Another one."

So, I made another. And another. As I waited for Saygar to finish his fifth burrito, I stared at my backyard from the kitchen window. It was difficult to see the entire yard since it was long and narrow. From the back door, you stepped into a lawn area. At the end of the lawn was an old wooden picket fence, and past that was an old barn. Behind the barn was my aluminum can recycle pile, a vegetable garden, a few fruit trees, and one giant cottonwood tree. Hidden among the branches of the cottonwood was a treehouse. Beyond the treehouse was the back fence and the train tracks. That's when I got an idea.

As soon as Saygar was finished with his burrito, I had him follow me out the back door. We walked past the lawn area, the wooden picket fence, the old barn, the vegetable garden, and the cottonwood tree to get to the treehouse.

"It's perfect. This is where I'm going to hide you...I mean...this is your home until you shrink back to ant size," I said. I scrambled up the ladder and called down to Saygar, "Come on up!"

I could tell by the smile on his face that he liked it. It was bright and roomy inside. Three of the walls had windows with views of the yard. I showed Saygar how to climb out of one window and crawl up one of the branches to see straight into my window.

"I can get us flashlights, so we can talk to each other. You know, like using Morse Code or something like that," I said.

We climbed down the ladder and returned with rags, a broom, and a bucket of soapy water. We scrubbed and swept every inch of the place. After we were done, we headed to my bedroom for additional supplies. I crawled under my bed and pulled out a box that stored all my finds from my hunting expeditions.

"Can you believe that people threw away all this good stuff?" I asked as I pulled out an old tablecloth, a pair of scissors, and a handful of twisty-ties. I remembered an old bean bag in

the laundry room that my mother had been wanting to throw out. We lugged the bean bag along with the other stuff into the treehouse. I cut the tablecloth into curtains and used twist-ties to hang them up. We cleaned up the bean bag and placed it near a window. "You can kick back and relax while looking up at the stars. Cool, huh?"

We sat back and looked at the stars for a while. I was pretty proud of my handiwork and quick thinking. From a distance, I heard my mother calling me. As I climbed down the ladder, I looked up at Saygar and said, "First thing in the morning, you meet me in my front yard. Got it?"

Saygar nodded, "Got it."

Chapter 7
Not A Dream

Early the next morning, I was wrapped up in my favorite fuzzy blanket when I heard movement in the living room. I figured it was my father leaving for work and didn't worry about it. I yawned and rolled over. I remembered that I had trouble falling asleep the night before, a nagging feeling in the pit of my stomach had kept me up. I scrunched up my face as I searched for the reason for my worries. My mind was cloudy with sleep to remember. I snuggled deeper into my blanket.

My ears picked up my brother Omar whispering to my other brother Eli in the living room.

"I tell you, that guy has been there for a while," said Omar.

"He's checking the house to rob us," answered Eli nervously. "Let's sic La Budget on him!"

La Budget was our family dog. She was small, black, and looked kind of like a poodle. She had wandered into our yard many years ago before I was even born. I had heard the story so many times that I felt like I had lived through it. The story was that our mother had not been pleased when Omar, a baby at the time, had opened the front gate and let a little black dog into our yard. My mother chased the dog out only to have Baby Omar let her back in. When my mother tried locking the gate, Baby Omar threw himself down on the ground and had a tantrum. His screams were so loud that people stared out their windows and cars stopped in the street.

My mother pleaded with Baby Omar. She told him, "It cost too much money to have a dog, baby boy. Think of la budget."

But Omar was a tough baby and stood his ground. So we got to keep the dog, naming her La Budget. Small, mighty, and old--La Budget was not the type of dog to scare anyone away.

"She'll have a heart attack before she gets close enough to bite him," said Omar.

I heard Eli yell, "Mom, call the police! There's some skinny kid wearing a hat trying to break into our house."

I bolted up. In an instant, memories of what happened the day before flooded my head. There was an ant, a big one. I put clothes on him. It hadn't been a dream. What was its name? I snapped my finger and told myself, "Something with an S."

I jumped out of bed and fell to the floor. My legs had tangled in my fuzzy blanket. I couldn't move. Sprawled on the floor, I wrestled with my blanket. I didn't have time to lose. With me tightly rolled up like a human burrito, I used my arms to scoot myself across the floor. Once I reached the hallway, I pushed myself up into a standing position and hopped the rest of the way.

"Don't call the police!" I shouted as I entered the living room. On my last hop, I lost my balance and fell. I looked up at my mom and pleaded, "Don't get him arrested!"

"You're getting those blankets dirty! I just washed them," complained my mother, freeing me from the blanket. "Why is your friend here so early?"

I shrugged. I peeked out the window to make sure it was the ant that was stalking our home. I was hoping I would get lucky and see an actual thief. Nope. It was the ant wearing the same clothes. I closed my eyes for a second and inhaled a lung full of air to calm myself. "It's him."

"Call him in. We can't have Saygar standing outside," said my mother. Noticing my blank expression, she added, "I was listening to you in the kitchen yesterday. His name is Saygar."

"*That's* his name," I thought as I slapped the side of my head. I opened the door and called Saygar in. I introduced him to my family. I studied their expressions looking for signs of fear, but they only looked sleepy. I thought it would be best to get things moving before they fully woke up. I ushered Saygar towards the kitchen and announced, "I am so hungry. What's for breakfast?"

"It's 6:30 in the morning," yawned Omar. He paused and agreed, "Yeah, what's for breakfast?"

We really didn't need to ask. We always had *huevos con chorizo*. A plate of scrambled eggs with chorizo and one tortilla was placed on the table for each of us. As I tore off a small piece of my tortilla to scoop up the spicy egg, an idea came to me.

"Mom how much does a *curandero* charge?" I asked, and I stuffed my tortilla scoop of egg into my mouth.

Since Saygar didn't seem to be *El Cucuy* or *La Llorona*, I figured that he was maybe an old-fashioned curse. The way I saw it, all I had to do was let the *curandero* do his magic stuff, Saygar would transform into a small ant again, and I'd be free. I had a couple of dollars in my underwear drawer and a 39-gallon trash bag filled with crushed aluminum cans worth at least ten dollars ready to be taken to the recycling place.

My mom laughed. "Why would you need to see a *curandero*?"

"Just look at his face, Mom. Of course, he's cursed," joked Omar.

"Ha, ha," I laughed sarcastically.

According to my mom, a *curandero* visit cost a lot more money than what I had. I would need a whole bunch of 39-gallon bags of cans to pay for the visit. Besides, she refused to let me waste my money. I was stuck with Saygar, a possible curse, until he shrunk back to ant size. I let out a big sigh and went back to eating my breakfast. I glanced at Saygar and could see he was struggling to eat his egg with the tortilla. The egg kept falling off his tortilla scoop.

"Here, use this," I said, handing him a fork.

He was not any better with the fork. Saygar spilled his egg on to the floor. In a split second, he was on his hands and knees stuffing the egg into his mouth. As quickly as he stuffed the egg in his mouth, he spat it out.

"Saygar doesn't like spicy food," I explained as I grabbed Saygar and pushed him back in his chair. He tried to return to the floor, but I held him firmly to the chair. I ignored the confused looks on my family's faces. "I guess we better get to school."

"*Mijo*, it's not even 7:00," my mother said and returned to the stove. "I'll make some more egg without the chorizo."

Another plate was served to Saygar who took a bite of the new egg. He pounded the table as he coughed and wheezed.

"Now, what's wrong?" asked Eli.

"I think the pan still had the chorizo flavor," said my mother as she rushed over to hand Saygar a glass of milk.

"Not milk!" I cried out and pushed the milk away. "Butter!"

The panic in my voice and Saygar's red face made Omar jump for the refrigerator for a stick of butter. Saygar chewed on the butter and calmed down. My mom and brothers remained standing, utterly speechless.

"I couldn't use milk, because it messes him

up. It makes his stomach all bad," I tried to explain.

"It makes him throw up?" asked Omar.

"Yeah. There's other stuff too. He's..." I paused as I thought of Irwin's words. "He's loco intolerable."

"*¿Que quiere decir, mijo*?" My mom placed her hand on her cheek. "What are you trying to say?"

I threw up my arms in defeat and cried out, "He toots! He does stink bombs when he drinks milk. Not the quiet ones. He rips them in a bad way. Big ... loud ... long ... and *stinky*!"

Saygar backed me up by nodding. My family was not sure of how to respond to this information. Normally, my brothers would have had a good laugh over it. They would have teased him and shown no mercy. However, Saygar was a guest in our home, and most importantly, our mother was giving them the "don't you dare" look. They kept their heads down to hide their grins.

Chapter 8

Funny Face

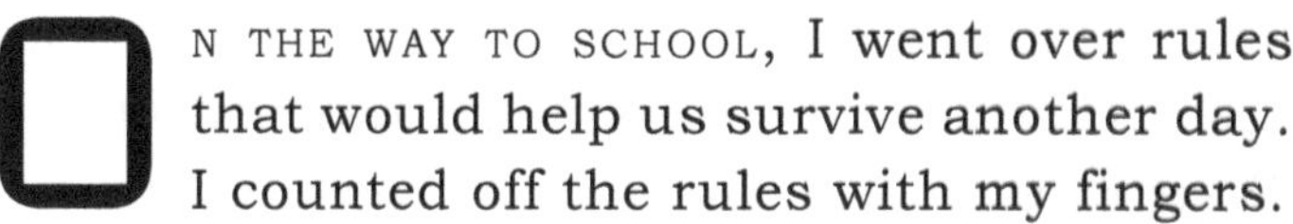

ON THE WAY TO SCHOOL, I went over rules that would help us survive another day. I counted off the rules with my fingers.

1. Don't say a word.
2. Keep your eyes on Ms. Kelly.
3. Keep your hands, yes both hands, to yourself.
4. No drinking milk at home, at school, or any place with people.
5. No stink bombs at the same places as in number 4.

I would have used all ten fingers, but we had already arrived at school. The bell was ringing and day two began.

The first hour passed quickly. Saygar followed the rules. He kept his eyes on Ms. Kelly. His hands rested on his desk. There was no chance of him getting milk in class. His memory of the rules got fuzzy by the second hour. He stopped looking at Ms. Kelly and sat playing with his fingers. To make things even harder for me, Marcie stared at Saygar, looking like a lion about to attack its prey.

Marcie raised her hand and said, "Ms. Kelly, Saygar doesn't have his math book out. He's not paying attention at all."

Saygar was told to get his book out.

On the pretense of needing my pencil sharpened, I stopped with Saygar to remind him to follow the rules. Saygar pulled out his book from under his desk. I stayed at the sharpener, slowly rotating the handle with my eyes on Saygar. By the time Ms. Kelly noticed me and asked me to return to my desk, all that was left of my pencil was the eraser.

As I sat back at my desk and refocused my eyes, I made eye contact with Marcie. She scrunched up her face and stuck out her tongue. I thought the face was meant for me, but that mean look in her eyes went past me to someone in the back. I followed her glare to Saygar. At first, it looked as if the face thing was going to be a one-time thing. When Ms. Kelly turned to write numbers on the board, Marcie did it again. A smile spread on Saygar's face. With Marcie still looking straight at him, he wrinkled his nose and stuck out his tongue just like she had done. Marcie frowned and shook her finger at him. I watched Saygar push up his nose, cross his eyes, and stick out his tongue. Marcie slammed her hands on her desk.

"My goodness, Marcie," exclaimed Ms. Kelly, who jumped at the sound.

"Ms. Kelly, Saygar's making ugly faces at me," Marcie complained. Ms. Kelly looked over at Saygar, who was looking in his book with a pencil in his hand.

"Saygar, do rule number one," I said as loudly as I could without Ms. Kelly hearing me. "Do number one."

There was a tap on my back. It was Lorenzo. With a worried expression on his face, he whispered, "Is he going to do number one in here or in the restroom?"

"What?" I asked. The worried look on Lorenzo's face surprised me. I paused, scratched my head as I thought about how serious he sounded. It came to me that all the craziness that had been happening since Saygar joined our class, especially the vomit stuff, had everyone nervous. I choose my words carefully as I assured him that I hadn't meant the bathroom number one. "It's a totally different number one," I said. With Lorenzo looking calmer, I turned my attention back to Saygar.

I waved at Saygar, but he completely ignored me. He looked over at the board to see if Ms.

Kelly was looking in his direction, and noticed she wasn't. He moved his eyes in Marcie's direction who was facing the front looking as if she was paying attention to Ms. Kelly. I knew she wasn't, and Saygar knew it as well. He waited ... he had figured out that Marcie knew what he was up to. She would turn around, and as soon as she did, Saygar was ready. He put his hands on his head, wiggled his fingers, squinted his eyes, and stuck out his tongue. He didn't wait for her reaction. He moved on to his next face. He pushed back his cheeks, pulled down his eyelids, and wrinkled up his nose. His face was so creepy that there was no need to stick out his tongue.

"He's doing it again," whined Marcie.

Everyone stopped working and looked up. Ms. Kelly looked over at Saygar, who was looking like the smartest kid in school with his nose in his book.

"Marcie, please keep your eyes on your work," was all Marcie got from Ms. Kelly.

Marcie glanced over at Saygar only to find him waiting for her. He did face after face. I guess I should have done something to stop him. I could have thrown myself out the window or fallen on the floor and pretended to faint.

I didn't, because it was like watching a train wreck. I had to look. Those faces were gruesome and awesome all at the same time. Marcie's reaction was another thing I had

to watch. Her angry face was just as spooky as some of Saygar's faces. Ms. Kelly turned around in time to catch Saygar stretching out his mouth with his fingers and pushing up his nose.

"Saygar!" Ms. Kelly gasped. "I am speechless."

"He's been doing that forever!" cried Marcie.

Ms. Kelly quickly found the words to say, with a loud and clear voice, "Saygar, you need to go to the Time-Out Corner."

The Time-Out Corner was a desk facing the bare white wall located at the back corner of the room. A student sent there was expected to sit quietly for a period of time, depending on how bad the offense was. I was there once for an hour and a half. The worst was Roger Vega, who I'm pretty sure was there for several days.

"Ms. Kelly, how long do I have to be here? What am I supposed to do here?" asked Saygar.

"You have to live there forever," said Marcie.

"Marcie, behave or you will be joining Saygar," warned Ms. Kelly. To Saygar, she explained, "You need to use this time to think about your actions and the bad choices you made this morning. You need to think about what you should have done differently."

There wasn't anything I could do for Saygar at that point. I had no choice, but to concentrate on my work. It was quiet for twenty minutes before Saygar startled everyone when he yelled, "I'm finished!"

"Inside voices," Ms. Kelly scolded. When she asked Saygar what he learned about his actions and how to improve, he answered in a whisper.

"I learned that I did not do a good job looking out for you. Next time, I will stop my faces before you turn around. Then, I will never get the Time Out Corner." Saygar finished with a smile.

A tight twinge in my stomach made me catch my breath as I waited for Ms. Kelly's reaction. In fact, everyone's attention was on Ms. Kelly's face. She drummed her fingernails on her desk as she thought of what to say. The nail drumming stopped. She cleared her voice.

"Saygar, I appreciate you using your inside voice. In this classroom, everyone must respect the rules. I am sad to see that you are not taking this seriously." I could see that Saygar was confused as Ms. Kelly continued. "It seems to me that you need extra time."

Saygar was to stay where he was for the rest of the day. We heard loud moaning from the corner for a while, and then silence.

Chapter 9

The Orange Mess

THE SILENCE FROM THE TIME-OUT Corner worried me. I peeked back to check on Saygar. He sat motionless in his chair staring at the wall. He looked tired. I watched him rest his feet on a nearby chair and lean back into a comfortable position. His cap slid back dangling dangerously from a wiggly antenna. With everyone bent over their work, I tiptoed over to the Time-Out Corner. A soft snore from Saygar told me he had fallen asleep. I peeked into his face and thought he looked so harmless asleep. Better to keep him that way, so I pushed his cap low to cover his antennae and tiptoed back to my desk.

At 11:30, I gently tapped Saygar's shoulder to tell him it was lunchtime. It took the full walk from the classroom to the cafeteria for Saygar to lose his sluggishness from his nap. By the time we sat down to eat our lunch, he was back to being fidgety. As soon as he was finished with his tuna and syrup burrito that I made for him that morning, I rushed him out of the cafeteria. I wasn't going to take any chances. We went outside and sat side-by-side under the farthest mulberry tree on the playground. I remembered I had an unopened package of grape-flavored bubble gum in my pocket and offered Saygar a stick.

"You need to take the wrapper off and..." Before I could finish my sentence, Saygar had already swallowed the entire stick, whole wrapper and all. He held out his hand for another. I shook my head.

"You're supposed to take the paper off, and just chew the gum. Don't swallow it," I scolded.

I gave him another stick of gum. He did the same thing again. When he poked me for another piece, I crossed my arms and refused.

"You gotta do it right. Watch and learn," I said. I pulled out a stick, held it out in plain sight, and unwrapped it. I put the gum in my mouth and slowly chewed. "See ... take your time ...enjoy."

I decided to get fancy. I moved the gum on to the tip of my tongue and blew a small purple bubble. Judging from the smile on Saygar's face, he was impressed.

"Let me try," he said. I gave him another stick which he unwrapped, slowly chewed, and blew. He blew the gum out of his mouth onto the ground.

"Don't worry. Blowing bubbles takes practice. Here," I said, placing the package of bubble gum in his hand.

"All this for me?" he asked with a grin.

"Just remember not to swallow it," I told him.

The blaring blast of the bell got us up on our feet.

"Race you!" I shouted, running towards the school doors. Saygar accepted my challenge and ran after me. It turned out that Saygar was a fast runner. He passed me in no time, leaving me far behind.

As soon as we entered the classroom, Ms. Kelly gave us a writing assignment to discuss "our aspirations for the future." Ms. Kelly was in a better mood after lunch and allowed Saygar to return to his desk. As I thought about my aspirations, I wondered if Saygar, or any ant, thought about the future. Could Saygar be more than an ant?

The clamor of the pencil sharpener startled me out of my thoughts. It turned out that Saygar had no thoughts about the future: the writing assignment bored him so much that sharpening his pencil seemed more exciting. He stood there, turning the handle as fast as he could, until Ms. Kelly's threat of the Time-Out Corner sent him back to his chair.

Saygar sat bent over his paper. He hadn't written anything. He spent his time gnawing on his pencil as if he was eating corn on the cob. With no pencil, since he ate it all, he looked around for something to do. He peeked at Ruby's paper but could not see through her long hair. On the pretense of searching for something under his chair, Saygar peered over Georgie Jr.'s shoulder. Georgie Jr. covered his work and made a face.

"I'm going to tell Ms. Kelly that you're trying to copy me," Georgie Jr. snapped and stared at Saygar, forcing him to turn away.

Saygar slid back in his chair. With nothing else to do, he reached in his pocket for his bubble gum. He glanced around to make sure no one was watching. After a quick chew, a small purple bubble emerged from his mouth. The frown on his face told me the bubble was not as big as he wanted. His cheeks puffed out. The lump of gum popped out of his mouth and landed on his paper like a purple slimy paperweight. He peeled it off and returned it to his mouth. He puckered and blew into the bubble growing from his mouth. It was the size of a golf ball--and clearly not big enough to his liking yet. He continued blowing: size of a tennis ball ... almost there.

Finally, the bubble was the size of his face. He looked up at me and pointed victoriously at the bubble. I gave him a thumbs up. He

swiveled cautiously in his chair, so I could get a side view. As he moved, the purple bubble began to deflate. I saw him huffing and puffing to save his bubble. As the bubble turned into a wrinkly lump, he gave one last, hard puff. The purple chunk of gum exploded out of his mouth straight into the back of Ruby's head.

Saygar slumped down in his chair. I looked to see if anyone had noticed. No one had. Even Ruby was too busy to feel the gum hit and stick firmly to her hair. I took a deep breath and decided the only thing for us to do was to ignore the gum thing. It was almost time for the bell to ring, and school would be over. Let Ruby deal with the gum on her own at home, far away from us.

Saygar went back to drawing and eating crayons. I did what I could to keep from thinking about the gum. I continued to work on my essay. I then avoided writing my essay by cleaning my desk and sharpening my pencil. After doing all that, the purple gum never left my thoughts. I had to get rid of it!

I made my way down the aisle. As soon as I reached Saygar, I hid under his desk out of Ms. Kelly's view. I reached up to pluck the gum out, but Ruby shifted in her seat. She yawned and scratched her head. The gum disappeared in her hair! As soon as Ruby stopped, I made another attempt. With my pencil, I moved a few strands of her hair out of the way and reached for the gum. When my fingers made contact, I tugged.

"Ouch!" cried Ruby.

"Joseph, what are you doing?" asked Ms. Kelly. Ruby along with the others in the class stared at me like I had ten heads.

"I was...looking for my pencil," I said. I felt my face turn red and my eye twitch.

"What's wrong with your eye?" Ruby asked, looking worried. I looked over at Ruby, who had no clue that there was a huge ball of gum in her hair.

"Nothing," I stammered and hurried back to my desk.

Saygar made the next move. He brought out a pair of scissors. We locked eyes, and I gave the nod. He prepared for the first cut. Ruby stopped writing and reached down for something in her backpack. As she rummaged, her hair moved, and I could see the gum was in plain sight. I saw the sharpen edges of the scissors move. Saygar slumped back in his chair. I closed my eyes and waited for some type of commotion. Hearing nothing, I did a quick peek over at Saygar, and saw him holding a chunk of Ruby's hair. He motioned that the gum was still stuck on her head. I shook my head and motioned for him to stop. Knowing Saygar, he'd leave Ruby bald if he cut any more of her hair.

"Where did it go," whispered Roger Vega who had sneaked over to me. Roger was a slippery type of kid. On one hand, he was sort of cool. He was tough, but not in a scary way. He was the only one that was good in sports, except for hula hooping. He was the only kid in third grade, maybe the whole school, that wore cologne. On the other hand, he was sneaky. If something went wrong in the classroom that had all of us scratching our heads wondering why it happened, it was probably Roger who did it. Like the time a bottle rocket mysteriously blew up in the lunchbox closet or the time the bathroom flooded because someone flushed a library book down the toilet. That was Roger. This sneaky, slippery kid had been watching us and the gum situation from the beginning.

"What do you mean?" I asked, feeling a little uneasy now with Roger involved. I picked up my pencil and pretended to work on my essay.

Roger smiled and made his way to Saygar.

I put my pencil down and watched. Roger said something, and Saygar pointed to Ruby's head. There was some more talking. I tried my best to hear, but they were too far. Roger pointed to a bundle under Georgie Jr.'s desk. A big bottle of orange soda was sticking out from Georgie Jr.'s backpack. Saygar stretched out his leg, hooked the backpack straps with his foot, and dragged it closer to himself so he could grab the bottle of soda. I saw Roger mouthed the words "shake it".

My heart pounded in my chest: something was about to happen. I felt it in every bone in my body. I should have done something, but I froze. Saygar gave the orange soda a few hard shakes and unscrewed the cap. On the last twist, I heard a hissing sound from the bottle. As soon as Saygar lifted off the cap, the orange soda pushed its way out of the bottle like a caged animal rearing its head, hissing and spraying a jet of venom. The orange stream hit Ruby on the back of the head. She squealed.

"Ms. Kelly, he's being bad, again!" cried Marcie. Saygar turned and sent a jet of orange soda into her direction. Marcie screamed.

"Drop the bottle, Saygar!" I hollered. Saygar pivoted around and squirted my face with the soda. I ran to him, wiping off my face with my shirt. I saw Ms. Kelly turn in our direction, so I hid under his desk again. By this time, everyone was out of their seats, jumping over their desks to dodge the orange stream. Saygar clung tightly to the bottle until it ran out of fizz.

"Saygar did it!" yelled Marcie triumphally. "He did all of this."

Georgie Jr. eyed the empty bottle and recognized it. "Hey, that's my orange soda!" he said angrily.

Ms. Kelly slipped and slid over to Saygar.

"Saygar," Ms. Kelly said while taking a second to compose herself, "Why?"

"I did it to save Ruby," Saygar explained. "That boy told me the orange stuff would take it off."

"Take what off?" Ms. Kelly asked. Before Saygar could answer, Ruby gave out a gasp.

"Excuse me, Ms. Kelly," Ruby said and pointed to her head. "There's something in my hair!"

Ms. Kelly walked over to Ruby and almost stepped on my hand. "Joseph, what are doing down there?"

"I ... I ...," I stammered. I couldn't think. "I don't know."

"Please return to your desk," Ms. Kelly said.

I got up. As I passed Ruby, I looked at her. She looked scared and wet as Ms. Kelly ran her fingers in Ruby's hair.

"I feel something!" Ms. Kelly exclaimed and moved some of Ruby's wet hair out of the way to take a look. "I can't see it, but there's something there."

Everyone crowded around Ruby hoping

to get a look at the thing in her hair. Marcie pushed her way to the front.

Marcie gasped. "I see it. It's purple! It looks like a big purple frog."

"I know what it is. It's the Madagascar hissing cockroach!" shouted Irwin from the back of the crowd. Hearing that, everyone pushed and shoved to get away from Ruby. Being on the short side, Irwin jumped up trying to get a look. "I call dibs on the purple cockroach!"

"Please, Ms. Kelly, get it out," cried Ruby.

Ms. Kelly called out for her bug spray and a ruler. Lorenzo held the spray while Ms. Kelly used the ruler to move the hair out of the way.

"Don't move, Ruby. Lorenzo, get ready to spray," Ms. Kelly said.

"I don't want a dead, purple cockroach in my hair," sobbed Ruby.

"It's going to be fine, Ruby," comforted Ms. Kelly. At that moment, I had to admire Ms. Kelly. Considering her fear of bugs, she was being very brave. "I see it. Ready, Lorenzo?"

Lorenzo nodded. Ms. Kelly moved closer to Ruby's hair. She stopped. She looked puzzled. She leaned closer and sniffed, "That's odd. I smell grapes."

"I didn't know that Madagascar hissing cockroaches smell like grapes!" Irwin exclaimed.

"It's neither a cockroach nor a frog," said Ms. Kelly.

By this time, Ruby was a big mess. Her hair had stiffened from the soda and there were orange streaks on her face where the soda had mixed with her tears. Her whole body shook with each sob. Ms. Kelly hugged her and told her not to worry. Using the ruler, Ms. Kelly poked at the gum just in case she was wrong. Satisfied that nothing in Ruby's hair could hiss or bite, she used her fingers to pull at the purple thing.

"It's...it's a..." Ms. Kelly said. She looked up. "It's gum. A rather large piece of purple, grape-flavored gum."

Ruby wiped the tears from her eyes and sobbed, "Are you sure, Ms. Kelly?"

"Yes, Ruby. Were you chewing gum?" Ms. Kelly asked. Ruby shook her head. Ms. Kelly folded her arms and cast a suspicious glance around the room. "Well, someone in here was chewing an enormous amount of gum."

"It was Saygar," accused Marcie.

Before Ms. Kelly could say another word, Ezequiel tugged at her sleeve. The purple hunk of gum, hissing cockroach, and Ruby crying was too much for his sensitive nerve problem. Ezequiel had had an accident somewhere in the classroom. He whispered, "Ms. Kelly, I can't find my Extra Box."

Muttering to herself about what else could go wrong, Ms. Kelly went in the closet to search for the pants. She came out shortly after to ask if anyone had seen Ezequiel's pants. No one had. I waited to see if anyone was going to notice Saygar wearing the missing pants. No one noticed. Ms. Kelly had no choice, but to send Ezequiel home to get another pair of pants. Ruby was sent to the nurse's office to see if they could get the gum out of her hair. Saygar was sent to the Time-Out Corner. And Lorenzo was sent to look for the custodian to clean up the orange mess in room 106.

Chapter 10

Fall Olympics

Ruby was sent home because of the gum. It took two janitors an hour to clean up the soda while the class stood out in the hallway. While we waited in the hallway, and without a single piece of evidence, Marcie accused Saygar of throwing the gum into Ruby's hair. Everyone believed Marcie. All of them said that Saygar was not only evil but mean.

It didn't matter to me that he did the purple gum thing. It didn't matter to me that he almost bit off Arianna's slightly large ears or was known as the kid who throws up on people. I stood by Saygar and defended him.

"Who needs them," I told Saygar.

The next morning when Ruby entered the classroom, everyone gasped. Her long hair was chopped off, replaced by a spiked, short do. She reminded me of a porcupine.

I nudged Saygar and asked if he saw Ruby. Saygar looked around. His eyes moved past Ruby. I pointed to her and said, "There. That's Ruby near the closet."

"Did the gum eat her hair? Saygar gasped, looking worried.

Before I could say a word, Ms. Kelly was leading the class to the gym to meet up with the coach. It was time for the Fall Olympics. Fall Olympics was an annual event where all students in the school competed in sports. The kindergarteners, first graders, and second graders competed in rope jumping, relay races, and hula hoop. The upper grades play some type of sport, like baseball or soccer. We sat on the floor of the gym waiting for Coach Dugan. I always felt that Coach Dugan was the scariest teacher in school. She was a tall lady with short brown hair who towered over everyone. She always wore a green school shirt neatly tucked into a pair of white shorts, with a pair of dark-tinted sunglasses perched on her head like large bug eyes. Around her neck dangled a whistle which she wasn't afraid to use.

Coach Dugan blew her whistle and yelled, "Quiet!"

She only had to say it once.

"Boys and girls, this Friday is our Fall Olympics. Third graders will take part in the competitive sport of flag football. This week, we will be preparing for the game. When I blow my whistle, you will quietly exit through the back doors. Let me emphasize the word *quietly*," Coach Dugan said and shot a look of disapproval at the usual loud suspects. "And remember, I want to see teamwork."

"Hate it," I grumbled once we were outside and far away from Coach Dugan.

"Why?" asked Saygar.

I explained to Saygar that our school was pretty small leaving little room for switching up classrooms or teams. I had been with the same group of kids since kindergarten, and year after year, we had always been the worst team in the history of Fall Olympics. From jumping rope to hula hooping, we just couldn't get it right.

The worst year was first grade. That was going to be our year for the big win. We were Ms. Peterson's Piranhas scheduled to hula hoop against Mrs. Valles's Mighty Pandas, a kindergarten class. That Fall Olympics, we marched into the field full of hope, waving our colored hoops. I have to admit we never practiced or even looked at a hoop before that morning. Who needs to practice? Everyone knows how to hula hoop. Besides, our competition was a group of booger-eating kindergarteners.

The booger-eating kindergarteners turned out to be adorable yet tough. When Mrs. Valles led the Mighty Pandas onto the field, the crowd exploded in a lot of “Ooohs” and “Aws”. That’s how cute they were. The cuteness of those Pandas hid the truth from us. They were there to win. They had worked hard the week before to beat the first graders’ butts.

The Piranhas and the Mighty Pandas faced each other. The crowd quieted. Coach Dugan blew her whistle and the hula hooping began. The Mighty Pandas’ hoops went around and around. The Piranhas’ hoops mostly laid on the ground. We couldn’t keep those hoops up.

Ezequiel was the first to fall. The nervous tensions brought about a “little accident”, and he was led off the field. A minute later we lost two more Piranhas: Arianna and her cousin Kimberly. Georgie Jr. never tried. He just stood there with his hoop lying on the ground. He was disqualified. One by one, for one reason or another, Piranhas walked off the field. When Coach Dugan blew her whistle that year, the booger-eating Pandas had kicked the Piranhas’ butts.

Ms. Kelly’s third grade Wildcats sat under the shade of a mulberry tree with the same annoyed, unhappy look on all our faces. Except for Roger, who was throwing mulberries into Ruby’s spiked hair. And Ezequiel, who sat with his back to us, had red, puffy eyes--strong evidence that a “little accident” was on its way.

“What’s going on here?” asked Coach

Dugan. "Let's show some spunk. Get out on that field."

Marcie stepped forward and lied, "Coach Dugan, we decided that I will be a cheerleader. I can cheer and get everyone spunky."

"Nope. Not happening," Coach Dugan answered. She ignored Marcie's pout and asked, "Have you picked a team captain?" We shook our heads. "Get it done. I want everyone, I mean everyone, out on that field."

With that, the whistle blared, and Coach Dugan walked off.

"I will be team captain," Marcie announced. "I am the smartest in Ms. Kelly's class. So, I should be the boss."

"You're not the smartest. I am," corrected Irwin.

Marcie rolled her eyes and crossed her arms. "Maybe you are, but no one likes you," she said.

"Irwin's alright. It's one thing to not like someone behind their backs, but to say it to their face in front of everyone is just wrong," I said, surprising everyone by speaking up. I turned to Irwin, "It's just that sometimes you talk too much and use all those big words that we don't understand."

Roger nodded in agreement. "Yeah, that's not cool."

"I was not aware that it was my vocabulary that was offending everyone," answered Irwin.

"See, there you go again," complained Roger. "Hey, I know a lot about football. I watch the Super Bowl every year, and I never miss a Cowboys' game. I should be captain."

That was good enough for all of us. We voted. Roger's qualification won him the team captain position. Roger stood up and said to all of us, "Football is easy, but we have a whole bunch of dummies on our team who all throw like girls." He spat on the ground, finishing his pep talk with, "You're all losers."

"Actually, some girls are good at playing football. In some places, they play on high school teams." Irwin said. I motioned for him to stop talking.

"I will be the quarterback," Roger announced, looking to see if Marcie was going to complain. She had lost interest and didn't care who did what. He clapped his hands and said, "Let's toss the ball to see how bad you are."

Of course, Roger was right, everyone stunk except for Saygar. He turned out to be kind of good.

Roger looked Saygar up and down. "Not bad, Saygar. Can you run?"

"He sure can," I vouched. I nudged Saygar who had been secretly tasting the football. He liked the earthy smell and the leathery taste. Saygar gave a quick nod and went on chewing.

Chapter 11

Game On

IT DIDN'T TAKE LONG FOR the week to end. Before we knew it, we were standing on the field waiting for the other team to start the Fall Olympics flag football game. There we were, Marcie, Ruby, Georgie Jr., Lorenzo, Irwin, Ezequiel, Kimberly, Arianna, Amanda, Martin, Saygar, and me. We might as well not be there, because Roger Vega was missing.

"There's Roger," shouted Lorenzo. I lookcd to where Lorenzo was pointing. There was Roger on crutches moving awkwardly toward us.

"What happened?" Marcie demanded as soon as he reached us.

"Messed up my ankle," he explained. "See how swollen it is. Cool, huh?" After listening to us moan and groan about the game, he made a face. "You guys are a bunch of babies. Go out there and mess around until Dugan blows her whistle. The game will be over. Then, you'll get your cookie."

Georgie Jr. pushed his way up to Roger and asked, "What cookie?"

"After the games, we always get a cookie with juice. The winners get two," said Roger.

The reason no one remembered the cookie was because we always ran off the field and hid in shame until the Fall Olympics was over. In fact, as soon as we walked on the field for this game, I looked around for the best place for me and Saygar to hide when we lost.

Marcie glanced around and asked, "Where are the cookies? I'm getting my cookie now." Georgie Jr.'s face lit up with the hope that he would soon be munching on a cookie.

"I said after the game," scolded Roger. He jerked his head at Georgie Jr. "You don't need a cookie. You have all those Twinkies."

"What are you talking about? I don't have any Twinkies," Georgie Jr. stammered, nervously backing away from Roger.

Suddenly, there was a parting in the crowd. We turned to look. Our eyes widened, and jaws dropped. It was Mrs. Howard and her fourth-grade class, the Barracudas. The Barracudas were the worst group of kids in the whole history of the school. They were bigger and meaner than most kids. The one that stood out among them was Javier Manuel Duran Jr., "The Moose." He was the youngest of six brothers yet the biggest one of all of them. He was *huge*. I don't think The Moose was ever a small kid. Someone told someone else who told me that The Moose started shaving in kindergarten. I don't know if that's true or not, but I wouldn't want to be close enough to him to find out.

Ms. Kelly could not help noticing the size of the Barracudas. She leaned over and whispered to Coach Dugan, "Coach, aren't these kids a bit big for my students. I know they're only fourth graders, but ..."

"Don't worry, Miranda. This is a no-contact flag football game. They'll be fine," Coach Dugan reassured Ms. Kelly.

"Who's Miranda?" puzzled Irwin. It was hard for any one of us to imagine that teachers had names like normal people.

Coach Dugan blew her whistle. "All right now. We have Mrs. Howard's Barracudas up against Ms. Kelly's Wildcats. Just a reminder, this is flag football. That means no tackling or rough playing. Let's have a good and safe game!"

She blew her whistle. The game was on.

We had practiced all week with Roger as the quarterback. With no Roger, we were confused. We argued about who should take Roger's place until Coach Dugan blew her whistle and yelled for us to take our positions.

We stopped arguing and scrambled around.

Ezequiel ended up in the quarterback position simply because he had the misfortune of standing in the quarterback slot at the sound of the whistle. I ended up being the one that hiked the ball. I hiked it to Ezequiel, but he missed the catch. Obviously.

"Hey, that kid just wet his pants!" hollered The Moose, pointing at Ezequiel.

Coach Dugan blew her whistle. Ezequiel shuffled off the field as the first casualty of this year's Fall Olympics. In a panic, we scrambled for better positions, like we were playing musical chairs. I pushed myself to the right. I was no longer the hiker. Saygar was

promoted to my old spot, and Ruby was the new quarterback.

“Hey,” greeted Saygar. He looked The Moose up and down and added, “You’re big.”

“Shut up,” snarled The Moose.

“Just hike the ball to Ruby,” I muttered to Saygar.

Saygar hiked it to Ruby. She caught it... and threw an impressive pass to no one. A Barracuda caught the football and ran to complete a touchdown. Another pass was thrown and landed next to Arianna. She burst into tears and ran off the field--the second causality of the game. By this time, Ezequiel had returned wearing a fresh pair of pants.

“Hey, the kid who wet his pants is back,” The Moose announced to his team. He looked down at Ezequiel. “Did they change your diaper?”

Ezequiel lowered his head and wiped a tear from his face.

“Oh, is the little baby crying? You need a new diaper?” heckled The Moose. Ezequiel wiped another tear from his face. I also noticed that boogers were dangling from his left nostril.

“I don’t think he wants to talk about his diaper,” Saygar said. I felt my chest tighten and sneaked a look at The Moose. He didn’t look happy.

The Moose turned to Saygar and glared at him. “What did you say?”

"He was talking to me," rushed out of my mouth before I could stop myself. My voice got kind of squeaky and my hands trembled. I was worried that if Saygar got beaten up, he'd lose his hat, and everyone would see those wiggly things on top of his head. "Maybe Ezequiel has a diaper on and maybe not. Who hasn't worn diapers? I wore diapers. Everyone here has worn some as a baby. Am I right? Huh?" I looked around for someone to back me up.

No one said a word. I had no idea what I was saying. I kept on blabbering about diapers, silently praying for the sound of the whistle!

"How come I never got a diaper?" Saygar asked.

Just then, Coach Dugan blew her whistle. On the next play, Saygar, Amanda, and I were pulled out of the game. Amanda, known for her ability to talk forever about nothing, sat next to Saygar. As soon as a person was within hearing distance, she would start jabbering. She was nice, but a little goofy--and was a huge liar.

In kindergarten, she said her dad was a rock star that traveled in a gold limousine. We believed her. In first grade, she said her dad was a scientist who had a laboratory in their attic. We believed her. In the second grade, her father worked for NASA. He was an astronaut who lived on the Moon. Every other weekend he would visit her in his spaceship. We were promised a ride on that spaceship.

We never got that ride. By then, we all had stopped believing. It turned out that Amanda's father was a garbage man. I saw him driving the big garbage truck one Tuesday trash day. He waved at me as the truck roared by. It was the coolest thing ever.

I guess she liked talking about her dad so much because she only saw him every other weekend since her mom and dad were divorced. That day was no different. She turned to Saygar and said, "I used to live in a castle with my father. He's a king."

Before I could stop Saygar, he told Amanda, "I used to live in an anthill. I'm an ant."

"Really?" squealed Amanda. "That's where my father used to live before he became a king."

"I never saw him," said Saygar.

"That's weird. He knows all the ants 'cuz he's the president of the ants," she explained. "He had a pet earthworm. His name was Roots."

"Did you hear that?" Saygar nudged me.

I pulled Saygar close to me and muttered, "Don't believe it."

"What about Roots?" Saygar whispered back. I shook my head.

We quietly watched the game for a few minutes. Anyone with eyes could see that the Wildcats had no clue how to play flag football.

"They're not even trying," I complained. The Wildcats were walking around the field doing their best to avoid any contact with the football. At one point, I saw Marcie handing over the football to The Moose as if she was handing him a burrito. Coach Dugan blew her whistle and called a time out.

"When is this going to be over?" moaned Marcie. "It's so hot."

"Yeah. I want my cookie," whined Georgie Jr. He noticed Roger munching on a cookie, propped up by his crutches. "Hey, how come you have a cookie?"

In between bites, Roger said, "None of you should get a cookie. You guys stink!"

We watched Roger munch his cookie and slurped juice in silence. When Coach Dugan blew her whistle for us to get back to the game, Roger yelled out, "Do something out there! I'm bored out of my mind watching you guys!"

Saygar and I joined the team while Lorenzo and Ruby sat down. Irwin stood in front of The Moose. The Moose sniffed and looked down at him. The hair on my arms stood up. I closed my eyes and hoped that whatever The Moose was up to had nothing to do with Saygar or me.

"You the kid with the diaper?" The Moose asked Irwin. I thought that was weird. Irwin and Ezequiel looked nothing like each other.

"No," Irwin said, looking up at The Moose.

The Moose continued to make a show of sniffing as his teammates laughed. "It smells like stinky stuff, like wildcat stink."

"No. I showered this morning. Maybe I

stepped on something," Irwin said and checked the bottom of his shoes. "See, nothing there."

I did a quick check on my shoes. Nothing there on mine either.

"I think it's you," The Moose told Irwin. He looked back at his team as they burst into laughter.

"Really," answered Irwin. "I smell something, too. I smell the scent of a decomposing carcass left out in the boiling sun after being soaked by torrential rain."

He sniffed, again. He pointed at The Moose and exclaimed, "Oh, it's just you!" He turned to me with a smug look and whispered, "Now that's a putrid stench."

My eyes just about popped out of my eye sockets. I could not believe Irwin did that. The stress of the game and the hot sun must have made him insane. Feeling pretty good about how clever he had been, Irwin raised his head to look at The Moose's reaction. Without any warning and as quick as lightning, The Moose bounced the ball into Irwin's small face. I heard a loud smacking sound as Irwin's head jerked back from the impact. The Barracudas laughed while the Wildcat's held their breath, waiting for the screams of pain from Irwin. We heard nothing. Without making a sound, he picked up his broken glasses from the hot ground, turned, and walked off the field.

Chapter 12

This Is Where We Fight

When Coach Dugan asked what had happened, The Moose told her that Irwin had fallen. No one dared to tell the truth.

"Joseph, was that part of the game?" asked Saygar. I felt The Moose's eyes on me. I shrugged and walked away from Saygar without answering.

The game continued. Nothing much happened until a long pass thrown by a Barracuda was caught by Saygar. When The Moose held out his hand for the football, Saygar bounced it off The Moose's head just like he had done to Irwin. Saygar caught the football as it bounced off The Moose's head and ran down the field. My whole body went numb. I wanted to scream for Saygar to run for his life, but I didn't have it in me to do it.

The Moose was caught by surprise, but only

for a second. He rushed after Saygar. Saygar stretched out his skinny legs and ran down the field staying out of The Moose's reach. I stood there in awe as Saygar ran by me on his way to the goal line.

"Leave it to Saygar to do something stupid," commented Marcie. Coach Dugan announced a touchdown...for our team!

For the next few plays, Saygar was a one-man team. He was running up and down the field, scoring points for the Wildcats. The Barracudas started to get angry, pounding and tackling him to the ground. They didn't care when Coach Dugan penalized them for unnecessary roughness.

"Are we almost done? I'm tired," complained Marcie as soon as Coach Dugan blew her whistle for half time.

"From what?" scolded Roger. "You haven't done anything." He was interrupted by squeaky rumbles. We all turned to look at Saygar. The noises were coming from his belly.

"Are you all right, Saygar?" I asked.

"Hungry," he said and rubbed his belly.

I turned to Roger and pleaded, "Roger, do you have an extra cookie for Saygar?"

"Nope," Roger answered and plopped the last crumb into his mouth. The others patted down their pockets to show that they didn't have anything to offer Saygar. Roger held up his hand to quiet the others, and said, "Shhh! I heard something."

We all stopped to listen. Roger held out his hand to Georgie Jr. and demanded, "Hand it over! Don't say you don't have anything."

"I'm doing it," grumbled Georgie Jr. He pulled a Twinkie from his pocket, but before anyone could stop him, he jammed the entire thing into his mouth.

We all stood around, confused. George Jr. just shrugged. Attempting to talk with his mouth full, he mumbled. "I'm hungry, too."

As he spoke, the Twinkie fell out of his mouth and landed on the ground. Saygar, it turned out, didn't have a problem with dirt and Georgie Jr.'s spit cooties. He picked up the dirty Twinkie and ate it. We were grossed out, but it stopped the rumbling in Saygar's stomach.

I was worried about Saygar. He needed help. I wasn't the kind of kid who liked to stand up in front of the other kids and talk. I was a no drama kind of kid, but that day I did something crazy. I stepped out of my "comfort zone" and gave a speech to the Wildcat team to help Saygar. I got my idea from a movie about the Spartans I had watched the other night. I told them about the battle between the small Spartan army and their enemy, who had thousands of soldiers in their army. The Spartans were doomed, but that didn't stop them from standing up and fighting. I pounded my fist into my hand as I repeated these words from the movie. “This is where we hold them! This is where we fight!”

“So, you’re saying we’re like the small army of Spartans,” said Irwin. He had quietly joined us on the sideline. We were happy to see him. We had assumed that he was in some hospital room, screaming in agony. Irwin was alive but looked awful. There was a dark red blotch on his face and his lower lip was swollen. He had what looked like the beginning of two black eyes.

“Spartans sound like ants,” Saygar said.

Amanda nodded. “They sure do.”

Irwin adjusted his broken glasses, now held together with scotch tape, and said, “Saygar has a point. Ants are fearless. They have no problem attacking an enemy that can be quite larger than them. Plus, it has been documented that ants have organizational skills.”

“Yeah, Irwin,” I coached. “We can pretend to be brave like ants or the Spartans, at least until the end of the game.”

Saygar did something I didn’t know he could do. He became that fearless ant that he always was. He used those organizational skills that Irwin said ants had and began to strategize our defense.

“We got stuff we could use to fake a good game,” he explained and pointed to Irwin.

"Just look at him. He's all messed up. He looks awful. But is he hiding and crying? No, because he's got guts. That's the sign of a true Spartan or ant."

I could see that Irwin was impressed with himself. He knew that he was a genius, but he didn't know that he could be as awesome as Saygar was saying.

"Look at Ezequiel," Saygar said, pointing at Ezequiel. "If I had weak nerves like him, I would be having little accidents all over the place, but he has only done it once. Keeping cool in the heat of the battle is a sign of a true ant."

Later, I found out that Ezequiel had been having his accidents throughout the game. He kept the other accidents to himself and stayed away from any players, especially The Moose, in case he was stinky.

Saygar motioned to them to huddle close. "Ezequiel, The Moose keeps asking about those diapers. Next time any Barracudas gets near you, you tell them you're going to have an accident."

"What if I don't need to?" stammered Ezequiel nervously.

"They won't know. When I give you the signal, just say it," Saygar said. He turned to Amanda. "Amanda, you're going to go out there and start talking."

"About what?" she giggled.

"Anything. Just don't stop talking," Saygar said. He looked at Marcie. "Marcie, you do your usual stuff."

Marcie crossed her arms and made a face. "What do you mean?"

"I think he means that you need to nag, and complain, and yell. And be bossy. You know, the usual stuff," explained Irwin.

"Hmph," was all Marcie said. For once, she was at a loss for words.

We put our hands into the circle. I whispered so only our team could hear. I told them we were going to get hurt just like Irwin, maybe get sent to the hospital. I let them know that no matter what we were going to do on that field, we were going to lose. But we needed to face our doom just like the Spartans and the fearless ants. This couldn't be another situation like with Ms. Valles' kindergarten Mighty Pandas and the hula hooping battle. This was where we'd fight!

"Hooray!" we shouted.

Coach Dugan blew her whistle and the second half of the game began. Saygar hiked the ball to Ruby. While Ruby decided on who to throw the football to, Saygar gave Amanda the signal to initiate "Operation Chatterbox," which put her into chatterbox mode on steroids.

"My dad used to play for the Dallas Cowboys. He was the best quarterback. After he won a billion Super Bowls, he became their coach," The Barracudas, like all true Dallas Cowboy fans, had to listen. They forgot to block Ruby, giving her the chance to pass the ball to Saygar who ran and completed a touchdown. Amanda just continued, "My dad used to be a rock star..."

Operation Chatterbox worked for a while. It gave us the chance to move the football close to the goal line. The Moose yelled to his team to ignore the blabbermouth and to pay attention to the skinny kid with the hat. Unable to throw the football to Saygar, Ruby threw it to Martin. Now Martin is a small kid who always wore hand-me-down pants from his older brothers, who were all built like wrestlers. When Ruby threw the football to Martin, he was struggling to keep his oversized pants up and missed the ball.

"Watch that kid with the spiky hair," yelled The Moose. The Barracudas were now after Ruby. They had caught up with her and had her surrounded. Saygar gave Ezequiel the signal. I named this strategy "The Big 'A' Operation."

From the field, Ezequiel's small voice cut through all the football commotion and boomed, "I'm going to have *an accident*!" Ezequiel stomped into the crowd of Barracudas who had overpowered Ruby. "I'm really gotta have an accident!" The Barracudas did not know what that meant and ignored Ezequiel. When I saw a worried frown on his face, I thought he was really going to have an accident. Then, he stomped his feet and yelled, "I'm going to wet my pants!"

Like the parting of the red sea, the Barracudas gave Ezequiel plenty of room. Ezequiel was unphased. He just kept roaring his battle cry. "I'm going to wet my pants! I'm going to wet my pants!"

Ruby threw the ball to Saygar, who made another touchdown. The Moose was angry, so he grabbed one of the Barracudas and demanded, "You stop that kid!"

"The kid's going to wet his pants and put stink on me," whined the Barracuda. It was

Hector Manuel Duran, The Moose's cousin. "My mom won't let me in the house if I stink."

The Moose snorted in anger and stomped off.

After a while, Ezequiel did have to use the restroom, but "The Big 'A' Operation" was a success. He left the field for a bathroom break feeling pretty good about himself. On the next play, a Barracuda threw a long pass in The Moose's direction. Saygar watched the football glide effortlessly across the sky. He ran behind The Moose and placed his hands on The Moose's back. He pushed himself up and over The Moose. As Saygar flew over, he grabbed the descending football and sprinted down the field to score another touchdown.

Everyone playing and watching the game went crazy. We were the Spartans. We were like ants. We kept moving forward.

"That's the way you do it, Saygar!" cheered Roger. He waved the latest doughnut he was munching on in the air.

"Just marvelous, Saygar!" screamed Ms. Kelly.

The next few minutes were brutal. We were pinched, pushed, and kicked. Coach Dugan blew her whistle for a time out to give us a minute to breathe. Roger limped over to us and said, "Stall for time. The score is close."

Before we could talk over strategy, Coach Dugan blew her whistle. Just as Saygar was about to hike the ball, Marcie cried, "Ouch! Coach Dugan, someone just stepped on my foot. It hurts really bad."

Coach Dugan blew her whistle and the game came to a halt. She walked over to Marcie who began to do what she did best. She complained her foot hurt. It was too hot. The goal line was too far. With her arms crossed, she stomped her foot (accidentally using the one that "hurt") and demanded water. Someone needed to move over. Someone needed to walk faster. It sounded so Marcie that I wasn't sure if she had initiated the "In Your Face Operation" or she was just being herself. Annoyed, Coach Dugan blew her whistle and the game continued. Marcie had done her best but had not given us enough time. Saygar had miscalculated Coach Dugan. Coach Dugan was not as patient as Ms. Kelly. She did not put up with Marcie.

The Barracudas had plenty of time to win a touchdown and beat up on Saygar. There in the middle of the field, The Moose had Saygar in a headlock with Saygar's hat barely hanging onto his head. Time stood still for me. Everyone was about to know the truth about the new kid. I closed my eyes and waited. From somewhere in the cluster of Barracudas, someone yelled, "Hey, this kid is loaded with Twinkies!"

I opened my eyes to see Georgie Jr. bolting down the field with Twinkies flying out of his pockets. My first thought was that Georgie

Jr. was a stingy liar. My second thought was that Georgie Jr. was a stingy *dead* liar. The Barracudas, including The Moose, were right behind Georgie Jr. and his stash of Twinkies.

"*Aaaah*! Blow the whistle Coach Dugan!" screamed a very scared Georgie Jr. as he ran down the field.

"Give them up, Georgie Jr.," I yelled. "They're not worth it!" Georgie Jr. refused to give up his Twinkies and ran on. I remember thinking that I had never seen Georgie Jr. run. It turned out he wasn't very good at it. It didn't take that long for the Barracudas to catch him. They shook out all the hidden Twinkies out of his pockets and left him sprawled on the ground covered in Twinkie wrappers. I named this unplanned situation "Operation Twinkie."

Operation Twinkie gave us what we needed. Georgie Jr. and his Twinkies used most of what was left of the game. We decided to just let the rest of the time run out. We agreed that we played a decent game, but it was now time to lose.

Saygar disagreed. As soon as the football was thrown, Saygar followed the flying ball. When the football was within reach, he jumped high and intercepted it from a Barracuda. I saw him scanning the field. I knew he would see that he was too far from our goal line.

Maybe he would see that we were right. It was time to lose.

He pointed at me. I was at the other end of the field near our goal line.

"Too far," I yelled. Saygar raised his arm, getting into a throwing position. Frantically, I waved my arms. "Don't throw it to me! Don't do it, Saygar!"

Ruby ran up to me, shading her eyes with her hands and squinting as she looked at Saygar. "I told him that you're too far. Get ready, Joseph! It's coming!"

I was not ready for this. This was one of those moments that I had always dreamed of: making the winning touchdown in the last few seconds of a game. The dream Joseph would catch the football and be the hero. The real Joseph was going to miss it. My chest tightened. It felt like my blood was turning into sludge. My heart pounded in my chest as it fought to squeeze the sludge blood through my veins. I thought for sure Ruby could hear the pounding. My arms went limp. I couldn't breathe. I gasped for air like a fish out of water. Inside my head, I screamed at myself, "Breathe! Just breathe!" The sludge in my veins was too much for my body.

My ears stop working. "Where is everyone?" I yelled inside my head. I couldn't hear the crowd anymore. Were they still there? My eyes opened wide. I felt myself spinning. I felt light in the head. Just when I thought I was going to drop in a faint, a single voice reached me.

"Catch the ball, you stupid moron!"

The voice could only have belonged to one person--Marcie. Any other time, I would have been embarrassed or angry. At that moment, when the fog took over my head, I kind of liked Marcie for what she did. I snapped out of it, wiped the sweat from my eyes, and looked up. I saw the football and moved into a catching position. I took a deep breath to steady myself and held out my arms. Wham!

"Ouch!" I stumbled and fell to the ground. The football landed not in my arms but had hit me on my head. With my face plastered to the ground, I felt the field vibrate as the two teams charged toward the football. I pounced on the ball, seeing it just ahead of me. I heard Coach Dugan's whistle. The game was over.

Chapter 13

Two Cookies and a Juice

COVERED IN SWEAT AND DIRT, I stood in the middle of the field with the Wildcats as Coach Dugan announced the winner. I took a deep breath. I felt good. The results of the games were not important. We never win. Thanks to Saygar, I could feel it in my bones that the score was going to be at least close.

"I first wish to congratulate both teams for playing an outstanding game," Coach Dugan said. She smiled at both teams. "The winner of the Fall Olympic Flag Football game between the Barracudas and the Wildcats is..."

She paused. We all leaned forward. "Folks, this year we have a tie!"

"What does that mean?" Saygar asked me.

"It means, we didn't lose," I shouted. The score was better than I could have imagined. To me, a tie was as good as a win.

"We didn't lose! We didn't lose!" cheered

Irwin. We joined Irwin in the chant. "We didn't lose!"

"I'm so proud of you," Ms. Kelly said and hugged us one by one. "You were just fabulous!"

"Miranda, did you see Saygar? He was totally awesome," laughed Irwin.

"I sure did. Saygar, you were magnificent!" Ms. Kelly cheered. "Irwin, are you okay?"

"Yes, Miranda," answered Irwin.

"Don't call me Miranda." Ms. Kelly smiled.

Georgie Jr. pushed Irwin aside to ask, "How many cookies do you get for a tie?"

It turned out that a tie got us two cookies and a juice. Plus, Ms. Kelly surprised us with a big box of glazed donuts.

"Hey, Irwin, did it hurt when The Moose hit you with the football?" asked Roger as we sat under the mulberry tree enjoying our sweet prizes.

"Yeah. It hurt something fierce," Irwin said with a grin.

"Next time you pick on someone that big, you need to keep your eyes on them. Never turn your back on them," advised Roger. "Also, you should learn to duck."

Marcie stopped munching on her glazed donut to point at Irwin's face. "Irwin, you have two black eyes. You look like a raccoon."

"Cool," Irwin exclaimed. He was pleased. The black eyes gave him the tough-guy look.

I showed off the big bump on my head

that I got from the football. It was not as cool as Irwin's black eyes, but I was proud of it. Everyone touched it and was impressed by the size of my *chichón en la cabeza*. We were all getting along, eating and laughing. Suddenly Amanda pointed at Saygar and shouted out, "Guess what? Saygar's an ant! He told me!"

All eyes were on Saygar. I froze and waited.

"Oh my gosh, Amanda," Marcie rolled her eyes. "The game's over. You don't need to make up stuff anymore."

"Amanda, when is your father going to give us that ride on his rocket ship?" I joked. When everyone laughed, I took a deep breath and

relaxed. This was all Amanda needed to forget about Saygar the Ant. She went on to explain that her father did not work on the moon, because he got a promotion. He worked on Pluto. It was too far for him to visit, and his rocket ship was in the shop. She would have gone on and on, but it was time for a group picture. With our messed-up hair, dirt on our faces, and stinky sweat coming off all of us, we turned to the camera and smiled. Click.

Chapter 14

A Promise is a Promise

IT WAS THE END OF the best day ever at school. Saygar and I were still feeling the excitement of the game. We couldn't stop talking about it.

"Did you see how Irwin's head whipped back when The Moose hit him?" In slow motion, I reenacted the moment the football made contact with Irwin's face.

"Did you see me jump over the big moose boy?" asked Saygar. Not waiting for an answer, he ran ahead to show me how he did it. As he jumped up, his pants slipped down.

"Keep those pants on," I laughed. I watched Saygar adjust his pants. He looked skinnier than he had that morning. I was about to tell him when I noticed something else. Not only was he skinner, but he was also shorter. "Saygar."

"Then, I grabbed the ball and...what?" he asked with his arm in the air.

"You're shrinking," I whispered, barely able to get the words out.

"Shrinking?" he gasped. I nodded.

Without thinking about it, we ran, not to the anthill but to the treehouse. We collapsed on the floor of the treehouse trying to catch our breath. We had been wanting this moment to happen for such a long time, but now that it was here, we had mixed feelings. In fact, I was wishing it would go away.

That best day ever made me realize how boring my life had been before Saygar came along. This last week had been like riding a roller coaster, screaming some of the time with eyes closed most of the time, worried of what was coming around the next corner, counting the minutes until all the craziness would be over. Like a roller coaster ride, I wanted to get on one more time now that it was over. We were not done talking about the game. We needed more time. A day like this calls for a minute-by-minute detailed discussion.

I scolded myself for being selfish. I had made a promise to Saygar to get him back to his anthill. In my family, making a promise was a big deal.

"Always think before you promise anything," my mother warned. "Once you make a promise, you do all you can to keep it. People have to believe in your word. So always remember, a promise is a promise."

When I made Saygar the promise, I meant it. I wanted it more than anything. But with him shrinking beside me, I changed my mind. I wanted him to stay.

"I think we're having pizza for dinner today," I said to break the silence.

"Aw," moaned Saygar.

Then, an idea came to me. "You could stay for pizza." If Saygar didn't want to go to the anthill, I couldn't force him. So technically, I wasn't breaking my word if Saygar didn't want to go.

"I could? How?" Saygar looked interested. Who could say no to pizza?

"I think it has to do with food. You probably used up all the food inside of you during the game," I said. "Just stay right there. Try to slow down the shrinking thing. Keep thinking big thoughts!"

I scrambled down the ladder and ran into my house. I grabbed at everything in the refrigerator, not caring what I got, and ran back to the treehouse with my arms full of food. I threw most of it into the treehouse and climbed in.

When I saw no sign of Saygar, I called out for him. I heard a noise behind the bean bag bed and slowly walked over to it. I didn't see anything. I squatted down. If Saygar was back to ant size, I would see him better close to the floor. I laid on my stomach, slowly moving my gaze from one side of the floor to the other. Something caught my eye. I blinked and stared. Something was moving. I squinted my eyes and concentrated on the spot. There was a small red ant.

"Saygar," I said. The force of my voice sent the little ant stumbling back. I covered my mouth with my hands and waited for him to get back up on his feet. As soon as Saygar recovered, I whispered, "I have your food. Come on and eat." I took a cracker and crumbled it near Saygar. Saygar crawled to the crumbs, waved his antennae, but didn't eat. I placed a chunk of cheese and poured syrup on it. Still, Saygar refused to eat. I was too late.

I felt tears on my face. For the first time in years, I cried. Being the youngest, I learned early on to toughen up. One sign of weakness and I'd be bombarded with teasing from my brothers. If they would have seen me up there in the treehouse crying, they would have been brutal. I kept crying. Not the quiet way, but the loud, shoulders shaking, boogies all over my face, type of crying. I didn't care.

I had no choice, but to keep my promise. The next day, I would take Saygar home. I stayed up in the treehouse until it got dark. From somewhere in the distance, I heard my brothers calling for me. The pizza was here. To keep Saygar safe, I gently put him back into my ant farm bottle.

I passed my family who were eating pizza in the kitchen and went straight to my room with my ant farm. I placed the bottle on my pillow and crawled into bed. I pulled the covers over my head to block out the laughter from the kitchen.

Eli walked into the bedroom.

"Hey, there's pizza, the good kind with Canadian bacon. *Abuela* dropped off a batch of *sopaipillas*. She just made them. Better hurry, sopaipillas are going fast," he said and poked me with his foot. "The pizza's getting cold."

Saygar would have loved sopaipillas, covered with all that sugar and cinnamon. He probably would have added a drizzle of syrup, I thought.

"Not hungry," I said through the blankets.

"Wasn't today the Fall Olympics? You guys totally made fools of yourselves and lost the game, huh?"

"Whatever," I mumbled.

"Mom wants to know if Saygar's going to eat here. She got extra syrup for him. Just make sure he puts it on the sopaipillas, not the pizza," Eli laughed. When I didn't answer, he gave me another poke with his foot. "Did you hear me?"

I kind of lost it then. I started to blubber, again. That got Eli nervous. He kept asking me if I was going to tell Mom that he made me cry. When I didn't answer, he left the room, closing the door behind him.

Early the next morning, with Saygar safe in the bottle, I crossed the bridge and entered the school grounds. I walked toward the sandy area at the far end of the schoolyard, went past the big slide, and stopped at the anthill behind the mulberry trees. I tiptoed over the busy ants and made my way to the opening of the anthill. It looked the same, but of course, it was not. It was missing one perfect ant. Or like Ms. Kelly called him, a magnificent ant. Back to blubbering, I stood there, a giant among the ants, getting boogers all over me and hugging the bottle. Saygar was not a curse or *El Cucuy*. Saygar was more than an ant that came to life. He had been a friend. No, I told myself. He was not just a friend but a great friend. In fact, he was a best friend.

Then, an idea came to me. Eating lots of food made Saygar grow, and having no food shrunk him. I knew the secret. I decided to give Saygar a few days to visit with his ant friends. Let him get strong. Then, I would put my plan into action. I'd call it "Operation Get Big" or maybe "Operation Getting My Best Friend Back".

I closed my eyes and took a deep breath. It was time to keep my promise. I tilted the bottle. Saygar slid down into my hand. I explained my idea to Saygar and gave my promise to return

for him in three days. I made it official by crossing my heart and pinky swearing.

"Saygar, you are my best friend," I said. I bowed my head and cried a little more.

I set him down with the other ants and watched him crawl away. I felt a tight knot in my stomach as Saygar disappeared down the anthill. I wondered if he understood me, wondered if he knew how important he was to me. It was going to be alright, I told myself. I'd see him again. There was nothing more for me to do, but to go home and wait. After all, I told myself, a promise is a promise. I'd be back. As I headed home, my stomach growled. I hoped there were leftover sopaipillas and pizza, the good kind with Canadian bacon.

ELIZABETH JURADO

ILLUSTRATED BY DAVEY VILLALOBOS

Chapter One

THE CUTE-AS-A-BUTTON MONSTER

I ONCE READ SOMEWHERE THAT THOSE spooky stories whispered in the middle of the night—usually during a thunderstorm, sitting around a kitchen table or in the middle of some creepy forest huddled around a campfire—should not be believed. It said we should trust scientists—that all scientists *know* it is impossible for ghosts to be real. They can't just trust their gut, these scientists would demand to be shown hard proof of spirits reaching from the grave to haunt us before shouting, "Aha! You can't because no such evidence exists!"

For a kid living in El Paso, the pointy nose of Texas, sometimes scientific logical words mean nothing. Sometimes things happen that have no scientific logic at all. Whether it's the Boogeyman or Slender Man—or for people in El

Paso, *El Cucuy*, or *La Llorona*—these old family stories sometimes beat out the logical thinking of those scientists. I am here to tell you that some of those mind-blowing, strange stories are real! I should know. I am one of those stories people tell around the kitchen tables and scientists don't believe in. One day EVERYONE will know my story. I'm not just a person who knows someone who saw something weird. I'm that someone who lived it!

My best friend was a *human-sized ant*!

Yeah, that's right! His name was Saygar, and he was an ant as big as me. He started as my show-and-tell project that turned into a whole lot of crazy! Was it scary? Sort of. Was it rough? Absolutely. When Saygar, dressed like a kid in a blue shirt, jeans, and high-top tennis shoes, first joined me in Ms. Kelly's third-grade classroom at Cadwallader Elementary School, I had to convince everyone he was normal. Then there was Arianna and her slightly large ear situation that caused a mess of trouble. And probably the worst was when Saygar drank milk and threw up all over Marcie in the cafeteria. It looked gross and smelled a hundred times worse. How was I to know that Saygar was "lactose intolerant"—something that Irwin, the smartest kid in school, informed me of after? As I said, it was kind of rough!

You know what really scared me? Not having

Saygar beside me where I could keep him out of trouble. That gave me the jittery shakes! The last time I saw Saygar was at the anthill in the far end of the playground, beyond the rusty old slide, and behind a group of mulberry trees. I had made him a promise when I first met him that I would find a way to get him back to his anthill. I did the cross-your-heart, pinky swear type of promise. Every kid knows that kind of promise was unbreakable. And I kept my promise! I got Saygar back to the anthill!

Of course, the fact that he had shrunk down again to a teeny ant and didn't fit in his human clothes anymore had a little to do with it. All the same, I had no choice but to take him back to the anthill because of my promise. But before I left him, I made another unbreakable promise. I promised I would come back for him in three days.

That was two whole weeks ago. I heard that when you break the unbreakable pinky swear promise nothing but trouble will follow you forever—until you do your promise. Forever is a very long time for a kid, so with that in my mind, I was a nervous wreck during those weeks. What kept me from keeping my promise? Let me tell you, it was something big, something that came at me without warning. It was a full force of nature, like a tornado or an earthquake. It was my four-year-old cousin, Julia Mateo!

Scratch.
Sccatch.
LA Budget

She LOOKED like a little thing in braids with big bows in her hair, ruffled dresses, and white strappy things on her feet that my mom called Mary Jane shoes. But don't let her small size and shoes so fancy that they have a name fool you. Julia was BIG trouble!

It's not that Julia was a brat. It would have made my life a whole lot easier if she had been. Everyone understands why you don't like brats! No, Julia was the opposite. She was adorable. She was cute. She was, as my mom would say, "Cute as a button!" That's what made her a monster. She had so much of that adorable stuff, that when she would do something wrong, nothing would happen to her. Some grown-up would get ready to give her a scolding, like she deserved, but look into her brown eyes and then forgive her for all her wrongdoings. It was like looking at a puppy, a rainbow, or a magical unicorn. They'd think what a cutie she was and that whatever she did wasn't honestly *that* bad. In fact, she'd get a smile and hug before she skipped away. Whenever I did something wrong, I never got smiles and hugs. I got punished, no way around it. But not Julia Mateo!

Sometimes, but not often, some grown-up would ignore this cute-as-a-button monster's weapon of adorableness and give her a good scolding. Her lower lip would quiver, her voice would shake, and the tears would fall. I must admit it was hard to watch. It was like watching a person kick that puppy, ignore that rainbow, or say that magical unicorns were overrated ponies. The grown-up would get the dirty looks and a scolding while Julia got hugs and kisses. Yeah, she was a monster to the core!

It turned out that the next day after I left Saygar at his anthill, this cute-as-a-button monster moved into my neighborhood, right next door to me. At first, I thought, along with my brothers Omar and Eli, that this change had nothing to do with us. Oh boy, was I wrong! Every time I opened the door to sneak out of the house to get Saygar, there was Julia, jumping over the fence that divided our yards to see what I was up to. It was as if she was a human motion detector set on my every move. I couldn't get rid of her, and as the days passed, I began to get antsy. I had to get Saygar back and soon! Not wanting to waste any more time, I decided to outsmart this monster. I planned to wake up extra early, sneak out of the house, and make a run for my school and save Saygar.

Early on a Sunday morning, I stood in the dark kitchen, not wanting to take a chance on turning on the light and Julia seeing it. Quickly and quietly, I checked that I had all my tools needed to get Saygar back. Twisty ties secured on my belt loop? Got it! Empty two-liter ginger ale bottle with some sand inside of it? Got it! Sugar cubes hidden in my left sock and a spoon in my back pocket? Got it! One more peek from the kitchen window to make sure there was no sign of the monster. Check! It was time for "Operation: Get Saygar Back"!

"Yeah!" I grunted softly and punched my fist into my right hand, ready to go.

I opened my backdoor and tiptoed out into the darkness. I slithered beside the shadows of my house, slowly peeking around the corner. No sign of movement. I got on my hands and knees to crawl around the rose bushes pausing occasionally to listen for any unusual noises. After I cleared the roses, I stood up and took a deep breath to steady my nerves.

"Ok so far," I whispered to myself as I brushed the dirt off my knees.

"Piece of cake, Jojo! Easy peasy," a voice in the darkness whispered back.

My heart thumped so hard in my chest I thought it was going to burst right through. I screamed, stumbled back, and fell into the rose bushes. I looked up and there stood the cute-as-a-button monster with *La* Budget, our family dog, at her side.

"Don't you ever go to sleep? I mean, really, when do you sleep?" I scolded Julia as I crawled out of the rose bush. I picked out thorns from my hand and frowned at *La* Budget. "Some guard dog you are."

As soon as I said that, I felt kind of bad.

La Budget, our small black poodle type of dog that we had for years couldn't help it. It wasn't her fault that Julia got past her. *La* Budget could barely hear, much less see. I knelt and hugged her. "Sorry, old Budget."

"Poor, *La* Budget! Right, Jojo? She's a good girl!" Julia exclaimed.

"Julia, call me Joseph!" I grumbled.

For some reason, she had trouble pronouncing Joseph when she was a baby. All she could say was Jojo, and she had been calling me that ever since. When she lived far away, I only had to put up with it on holidays, so I learned to live with it, but with her living next door, soon to be in pre-school at *my* school, that name was going to be a problem.

"Piece of cake, Jojo! Easy peasy, Jojo," Julia squealed happily.

"Aw!" I sighed in frustration as the cute-as-the-button monster began to skip around me and sing.

Chapter Twelve
THE TARANTULA TROUBLE

WE FILED OUT OF THE foul-smelling closet and back to our desk glancing nervously at the floor, searching for the escapee. While Ms. Kelly spoke about fractions, we pulled out our rulers for protection against a possible Big Herman attack.

Ms. Kelly had her back toward us as she drew a picture of a pie explaining how it could be divided into equal parts. I snuck a look over to Saygar and saw that he was still munching on crickets. Looking around to see if anyone else was watching him, I spied Marcie leaning out of her seat, eyeing the floor around her. I covered my mouth to hide my smile. It felt good that something else was bothering Marcie besides Saygar. I was about to draw a pie on my paper when I saw Marcie flinch in her seat. She began to frantically point at Ms. Kelly. I looked over to Ms. Kelly and my jaw dropped to the floor. I snapped around to see if the others had noticed and found them also staring at Ms. Kelly. What we saw gave all of us the heebie-jeebies!

There was Big Herman!

On that day, Ms. Kelly arrived and draped her favorite blue fuzzy sweater over her chair. While drawing on the board, she had put her sweater back on. Big Herman had somehow made his way to Ms. Kelly's desk and climbed up the sweater. His hairy legs were like Velcro on it.

From the back of the room, Arianna began to whimper which quickly grew into uncontrollable sobs. Every time she looked up to see the big hairy spider on Ms. Kelly's back, her sobs got louder. We tried to hush her, but she wouldn't stop. Ms. Kelly finally turned around.

"Arianna, what's wrong," Ms. Kelly asked. She looked around at all our faces and saw the terror. She clutched her throat and whispered, "What's wrong?" I waited for someone to tell Ms. Kelly the news, but no one wanted to do it.

"Ms. Kelly," I said in a low voice so as not to startle Big Herman, "He got out of his cage."

"Oh my goodness," Ms. Kelly exclaimed. She reached out for the drawer where she kept her giant bug spray.

"Don't move," I warned her. Ms. Kelly took in a sharp breath and froze.

"Where is he?" Ms. Kelly whispered.

Ms. Kelly

Without saying a word, we all pointed straight at her. She began to look behind her, but when everyone cried out, she stood still, hardly breathing.

I got up and slowly walked over to her. I stood in front of Ms. Kelly, looked her in the eyes, and said as calmly as I could, "Ms. Kelly, don't make any sudden moves, okay...Big Herman is not behind you...." I stopped, trying to figure out how to say it, deciding to do it quickly, like ripping off a bandaid. "He's stuck on your back."

Everyone was leaning forward, watching, and waiting. Other than her face turning white, I didn't see any signs of panic. Just when I thought Ms. Kelly was taking it better than we expected, Ms. Kelly let out the loudest screeching scream. She bolted for the door, tossing any desk that came between her and the door to the side as we followed closely behind her. She had this wild look that I had never seen before. I would not have been shocked if she had just plowed through the walls to get to the hallway. All the chair tossing and jumping loosened Big Herman's grip from Ms. Kelly's back. He plopped to the floor with a thump and raced away, arriving at the door before us. The panicked rush to the door came to a sudden halt...

GLOSSARY

abuela - grandmother

chichón en la cabeza - bump on the head

curandero - a healer who uses folk remedies.

El Cucuy - Mexican version of the boogeyman.

¿Eres estudiante nuevo aqui? – Are you a new student here?

huevos con chorizo - eggs with chorizo

La Llorona - Mexican ghost story of a woman seen weeping near a body of water.

limpia - a spiritual cleansing ritual of body,

mijo - my son

¿Que quieres decir, mijo? – What do you mean, my son?

sopaipilla - a puffy piece of deep-fried dough sweetened with sugar or honey.

Tía - aunt

About the Author

ELIZABETH JURADO IS THE AUTHOR of the Saygar Books Series. Elizabeth released her debut book, *Saygar the Magnificent*, in 2019, and a year later released *Saygar the Superhero*. After working in the Educational field as a substitute teacher and a first-grade teacher, Elizabeth plunged into the challenging role as a stay-at-home mom. Using her experiences as a teacher and a mother to three energetic sons who kept her on her toes, she was inspired to write her adventurous tale of a shy boy and an overgrown ant. Elizabeth is living in Texas with her family and three cats.

Readers will enjoy listening to *Saygar the Magnificent* Audiobook! Follow Elizabeth Jurado on Facebook at Elizabeth Jurado Author | Facebook and @Saygarbooks on Instagram.

About the Illustrator

Davey Villalobos resides in El Paso, Texas. He's been drawing and doodling since he could hold a crayon. Baker by day, illustrator by night, cyclist in between. Influences include Dr. Seuss, and many comic book artist favs such as Jack Kirby, Sam Keith, and Frank Miller. Music always plays into his art, from Radiohead to Slayer... The only thing more important than drawing... His family, especially his nieces Avery and Eleya. Instagram @ uncledaveydraws @lord_darth_baker

Acknowledgements

I wish to take the opportunity to gratefully acknowledge the assistance and contribution to several individuals, without whom the completion of my book would not have been possible. First and foremost, I would like to thank Lisa Caprelli. Without Ms. Caprelli's experience, guidance, and never-ending generosity, Saygar's story would still be in a cardboard box hidden in my closet. Thank you to the creative skills and imagination of Davey Villalobos who took my written words and brought Saygar to life. Thank you to Rebecca Koch, whose editorial skills and helpful directions were essential in bringing the book together.

I also want to express my deepest gratitude to my family for their encouragement, patience, and perseverance throughout the many years. Thank you, Mom and Samuel, for all your help in editing my drafts, so many I lost count! You are truly Saygar's number one fans. Nathaniel, thank you for trying to bring me out of the prehistoric typewriter era into the modern day of computers, google docs, and all that other technical gibberish. I'm a work in progress so don't go too far, I still need you. Thank you, Richard, for your support and analytical editing of the expertise of a seasoned teacher. Thank you, Dad and Andrew for your support. To Reyes and Priscilla, your professional input was greatly needed and appreciated. To Rudy and Liz, thank you for your support and advise despite your extremely busy schedule.

Finally, thank you to all the children I met as a student teacher, a substitute teacher, and a first grade teacher who inspired me to write Saygar's story.

Thank you to each one of you.

www.ingramcontent.com/pod-product-compliance
Lightning Source LLC
Chambersburg PA
CBHW030335310726
48979CB00001B/36